The Handicapper's Handgun

The Handicapper's Handgun

*To Dorothy
Best Wishes
Gerald B. Garner*

Gerald B. Garner

Copyright © 2012 by Gerald B. Garner.

ISBN: Softcover   978-1-4691-5813-6
         Ebook   978-1-4691-5814-3

All rights reserved. No part of this book may be reproduced or transmitted in any form or by any means, electronic or mechanical, including photocopying, recording, or by any information storage and retrieval system, without permission in writing from the copyright owner.

This is a work of fiction. Names, characters, places and incidents either are the product of the author's imagination or are used fictitiously, and any resemblance to any actual persons, living or dead, events, or locales is entirely coincidental.

This book was printed in the United States of America.

To order additional copies of this book, contact:
Xlibris Corporation
1-888-795-4274
www.Xlibris.com
Orders@Xlibris.com
111216

Begin reading

✓ PROLOGUE

The story of two men. Both retired police officers who had served most of their careers together. They had saved each other's lives on more than one occasion.

Both had reached the rank of sergeant before their retirement.

They grew up on Minnesota farms and had horses for pets. This led them to like handicapping race horses at Canterbury Park. Minnesota's race track.

One of the officers suffered a terrible loss when his only family, a son who was attending college is shot to death when he was caught between two cars full of rival drug gangs while fueling his car.

This led his father to take revenge. The people he had spent years arresting now must pay. And pay they did, again and again.

Cont. on pg. 11

ACKNOWLEDGMENTS

Thanks to Bill Arlt for letting me tap into his vast gun knowledge.

Bill knows his guns and is also a fine shot. Many a western prairie dog has found that 250 yards does not guarantee a miss.

CHAPTER 1

THE HANDICAPPER'S HANDGUN

As usual on a Friday night, I was on the hunt. I was parked in a lot in front of a shopping center. I was at a busy intersection of University and Snelling Avenues in what is referred to as the midway area of St. Paul.

I was parked near a bank in one corner of the lot. Behind me was the bank and to my right, a string of retail shops. Off to the other side was a McDonald's.

About in the middle of the lot, there was a car parked that I was interested in. I had worked this lot for several nights while switching cars so as not to be noticed.

They liked to park in the center of the lot so they could see cars enter the lot from any direction. It also gave them time to leave if they saw trouble coming.

The driver was the dealer and always had the bodyguard with him. His dope selling runners would come to the car to get resupplied with drugs when needed. I did notice one thing that was repeated every night. About 11:00 pm the bodyguard would leave the car and walk to McDonald's for food and drinks.

This was to be their fatal mistake. I waited and about 11:00 the bodyguard got out and walked to McDonald's, as usual. I got out and approached the car toward the passenger side. He was sitting resting his head back listening to some Rapp music. I held my silenced .45 down against my leg and rapped on the half-open window with my other hand. His head snapped around toward me as he said, "What the hell?"

11

I said, "For my boy, Buddy," and shot him twice in the face. I quickly walked around to his side and opened the door carefully, due to it being bloody from his head. I pushed him over and went through his pockets. I found little but then noticed the pouch on the floor. It was full of cash and packets of drugs. I took the cash. A children's home would be receiving a nice gift in the mail in a day or two.

I walked back to my car and waited for the bodyguard. In about 5 minutes, the bodyguard appeared with the food bag and walked back toward their car. About 50 feet from the car, he noticed there was no one sitting behind the wheel.

I walked back to my car and waited for the bodyguard. In about 5 minutes, the bodyguard appeared with the food bag and walked back toward their car. About 50 feet from the car, he noticed there was no one sitting behind the wheel. He stopped and drew out a gun. Looking around, he walked toward the car. He looked in the passenger side, and I could see his mouth moving as he placed his drinks and food on the roof of the car.

Then to my surprise, he pulled his boss's body out of the car and went through his pockets. Then he walked around to the driver's side and started to get in. Almost like an after-thought, he got back out, walked around and got the food off the car roof. He got back in and drove toward the lot exit to University Avenue. When he got there, he proceeded to eat a burger.

"Waste not, want not," I said to myself as I started my car and drove to the nearest pay phone. I called the police and told them where they could find a dead body.

I headed home knowing 1 more dealer was out of business and thought to myself, "That was for you, Buddy."

I shoot hollow points that I drill out myself. Since retiring, I work part time in a couple of sporting goods stores. Hollow points shatter and are hard to get barrel markings from for comparisons.

My gun, an old government issue Colt model 1911, has been my favorite since my military days. I've made a few changes such as the extended, threaded barrel to hold my home-made silencer.

The .45 has proven itself lots of times in combat. One example is on October 8, 1918, a small group of soldiers was ordered to out-flank a German machine gun position.

They soon found themselves under intense machine gun fire, losing a lot of men and leaving a Corporal York in charge. He was armed with an Enfield rifle and a .45. He made every shot from the Enfield count.

The Germans counted his rifle shots and after 5, they charged. York pulled his .45 and advanced in front of his remaining men toward them, reloading his .45 as he advanced.

The result was he received the Medal of Honor and was given credit for killing 25 Germans.

HOW ARABIAN HORSES CAME TO BE.
FROM ANCIENT BEDOUIN LEGEND.

AND GOD TOOK A HANDFUL OF SOUTH WIND
AND FROM IT FORMED A HORSE.

SAYING,

I CREATE THEE, OH ARABIAN,
TO THY FORLOCK I BIND VICTORY IN BATTLE.

ON THY BACK, I SET A RICH SPOIL
AND A TREASURE IN THY LOINS.

I ESTABLISH THEE AS ONE OF THE GLORIES OF THE EARTH.

I GIVE THEE FLIGHT WITHOUT WINGS.

CHAPTER 2

Just about every Saturday morning, I'd meet my buddy, Stan at a bar called the Country Lounge. It was a place where Stan and I would study the Daily Racing Form and plan our bets for later in the day at the local horse track, Canterbury Park.

It was the usual Saturday morning routine. The bartender, known only as Cat, was behind the bar tending to the early morning drinkers. Stan was in his usual spot at the end of the bar waiting for me, Elroy Sutton.

The racing form in front of him on the bard is the Bible for all serious handicappers. Cat, the bartender, was a handicapper-want-to-be. He was under our tutelage to become a winning handicapper.

He couldn't get over how Stan had picked the winner in the Belmont that was run last weekend. "Okay," he said, "I don't understand. Your horse didn't do crap in the Derby, so how did you figure he would win the Belmont?"

Stan replied, "Forget the Derby. As I told you, forget mud races unless you see in the racing form the horse does well on mud. The Derby was mud."

Cat replied, "Well, if it rains next year for the Derby, my money stays in my pocket."

I had explained to Cat that part of handicapping was to develop a system of money management while betting. Over time, I had developed a system and made myself stick with it. On short odds, I made a win bet, then I double that bet to place.

Some handicappers prefer to exacta or exacta box bet instead of place betting. I also exacta box bet if I really like 2 horses to win. In a case of 3 good horses in a race, I will trifecta box bet. That means they finish in the first 3 positions, but in any order. You want the longest-odds horse to finish first for the biggest payoff.

15

It had become a tradition for me to lay a horse racing fact on Cat every Saturday. A lot of the morning drinkers also looked forward to it.

I called Cat over. I always spoke loudly so the whole bar could hear. "Cat," I said, "Did you know a horse named Donerail won the Kentucky Derby in 1913 and paid 91 to 1? And would you believe the jockey's name was Goose?"

That got a chuckle out of the bar patrons and Cat. "Where do you get all this crap," Cat asked?

"I am a serious handicapper and I do my homework," was my usual sarcastic reply.

A few minutes later, my good friend and past partner at work came in and sat down next to me. We had worked together for years and both retired from the St. Paul police force. He had saved my bacon on more than 1 occasion, and I had returned the favor a number of times.

Elroy had not meant to retire when I did but his boy, Buddy, was killed. He was killed by a stray bullet when 2 car loads of dope-selling punks had a shoot-out. It happened in a gas station where Buddy happened to be fueling his car.

Elroy looked uptight, but after a couple of beers, he relaxed. We started to look over the Daily Racing Form when 1 of the guys sitting at the bar asked, "Why don't you just bet the favorite in every race? Doesn't the favorite win the majority of the time?"

I replied, "Actually, the favorite wins about 32% of the time. Of course, that varies by type of race, but only by a few percentage points."

"The betting odds are determined by the betting pools. The more bets on a horse brings down the odds. The problem is the betting public is wrong 66% of the time. Straight win bets will give you a loss of 8 to 11%. Believe it or not, to make a 20% profit at the track, you must win 30% of your bets at average odds of 3 to 1. To win 50% of your bets, the odds average can be no lower than 7 to 5." With that said, Elroy and I left for the track.

CHAPTER 3

On the way to the track, we were listening to the news on the car radio when our day was shattered! The radio said there had been a shooting at Regions Hospital in St. Paul. A Dr. Clark had been shot. He apparently was the intended target and had suffered a serious wound to his arm but was expected to recover.

This was the Dr. who had saved Stan's life a while back. He had suffered a major heart attack and this Dr. performed emergency open heart surgery and, no doubt, saved his ass.

The radio station had sent someone to the hospital to report live. He said the Dr. had been very lucky because his car had numerous bullet holes in it. Also, there was no doubt there had been more than 1 assassin. We wondered who in the hell would want to kill Dr. Clark. This was a good man who had saved lots of lives.

We got to the track 15 minutes before the first race and, as usual, the first race was a maiden race. Maiden means they had never won a race before. I've always said, "God couldn't pick the winners of maiden races and make any money."

Part of my betting management plan was to small-bet maiden races or pass on three-year-old maidens. After all, 3 years and still haven't won!

I decided to bet this maiden race and actually bet a three-horse trifecta box. Then I put these 3 with my pick in the second race for the daily double.

I did win the first race and, as luck would have it, the longest odds horse of the 3 I had bet on came in first. Now if my pick in the second race wins, I should pick up a nice payoff for the daily double.

I decided to put Cat's ten bucks on my pick in the second race. Then at the last minute, I put $20 more on him to win. Damned if he didn't get beat at the wire! There went Cat's $10.00 and my $20.00. Thank God I had won the trifecta to cushion the blow.

The 8th race was the big race of the day, a 1 mile race. An allowance race paying enough to bring in 2 shippers from other tracks.

As I always do, I eliminate all the horses I felt were out-classed. That left me with a field of 4 to be considered. I really did like 1 of the shippers. He had won the last time out at the same distance. Also, he had finished in the money for 3 races before that. But best of all, he had the highest Beyer speed rating than the rest of the field by 10 points.

I put $20.00 on him to win.

The Beyer speed ratings run from 1 to 115 plus. It is one of the handicapper's most useful tools. It first appeared in the Daily Racing Form in 1992 and quickly became very popular with not only the horse betters, but owners and trainers also.

The Beyer rating of over 115 is the best horses running today. A rating of over 100 is good allowance or stakes running horses. Ratings in the 80s are usually about a $10,000 claimer. Ratings below that are usually unclaimed or maidens.

Well, they are off in the 8th race and my shipper won it by a neck and paid $4.60 to win. I picked up my winnings and, due to the last race being a maiden race with no outstanding horses, we decided to leave.

We decided to hit the Mystic Lake Casino that is close to the track. It has a great card room and lots of Texas Holdum (my game) is played. We played till about midnight and headed out.

Elroy dropped me off at the Lounge to pickup my car and I went home. When I got there, a message on my machine said to call the Bail Bondsman that we occasionally work for. It being so late, I waited till morning to give him a call. I called and it seems a man out on a pretty good-sized bond had failed to appear for a court hearing. I told the Bondsman I would take the job of finding this guy.

My first move was to go to the house the Bondsman told me the guy rented. I picked the lock and got in. There wasn't much there. I found nothing to give me a clue where he had gone.

One of his neighbors did give me a tip about his hanging out at a nearby bar, a place called O'Gara's on Snelling Avenue. If you want information about someone who drinks, check with the bartender. I headed for the bar.

I walked in and ordered a drink. When the bartender brought it, I asked him, "Have you seen Bill McFalls?"

He replied, "Yes, a few nights ago."

"Did he say anything about leaving town?" I asked.

I noticed he got a wary look on his face and he asked, "Why are you looking for him?"

I said, "Well, we spent a little time together and I heard he was looking for work. The guy I work for is going to be putting on some more men. I figured Bill would jump at the chance. I know work is a little hard to come by these days."

That seemed to relax the bartender. He said, "I had to ask. I didn't want old Bill to get into trouble or have any problems on my account."

"Well, do you know where I can locate him?" I asked.

"I think so," he replied. "He said he was going up to his hunting shack in St. Louis county to do a little roof repairing. I doubt if he has a phone up there and I don't think he has a cell phone."

I asked him if he knew where the place was and he did. I asked if he would draw me a map and told him Bill would appreciate it because this might be the break he needs.

He drew a map showing me the way to the cabin. I thanked him and left him a nice tip. Like I said, "If you want info, check with the bartender."

I called the Bondsman and he told me to come and pickup the Warrant and paperwork on Bill McFalls.

I than called the Sheriff's office in the county where the cabin was located. I told them who I was and what I was going to do.

The Sheriff's office said they would call me back. Ten minutes later they called. They had checked my story with the proper authorities and gave me the go ahead. They also said if any problems occurred to call them right away and the officer in that area would respond.

Next I called Elroy and asked if he wanted in on this pickup. He did. I picked him up about 9:00 the next morning and we headed north on Highway 35. I had checked my map and figured it to be close to 200 miles to his cabin.

We both had a license to carry a firearm. I carried my .38 automatic and Elroy always had his favorite old .45 that he had carried for years. I bet every part of that gun had been replaced once or twice. I have to admit, on the pistol range, he was always right on with it.

We stopped for lunch about 12 miles north of Duluth at a place called Island Lake. I asked the bartender how far it was to the Brimson Road. He figured 12-15 miles.

We got to the Bimson Road and turned right, or east, at about two 0'clock. We had to go slow and watch for car tracks going off to the right because the bartender at O'Gara's had told us the shack could not be seen from the road.

About a mile and a half in, we saw fresh tracks going through the low brush to the right. A vehicle had entered and left a number of times.

We left the car near the road and walked in slowly for about 200 yards when we saw the cabin and a pickup truck.

Talking it over, we decided Elroy should circle around to the other side of the cabin. I gave him a few minutes to get in place. Then I walked to about 50 feet from the cabin door.

I stood beside a good sized maple tree. I figured if any shooting started, I could use the tree for cover. I called out, "Hello the cabin."

I heard a noise like a chair being slid across a wooden floor. Then the door opened and a man stuck his head out. He fit Bill McFall's description perfectly.

"What the hell do you want?" he asked. He stepped out of the cabin door leveling a shotgun at me. "Like I said, what the hell do you want?"

"I'm here to take you in," I replied. "Now can we do this the easy way or the hard way. It's your decision."

"Tell you what I think," he said. "You're a stupid fool coming up here alone to take me in. Now step away from that tree."

Then he heard the metallic click of a gun being cocked. He turned his head toward the sound and was looking down the barrel of Elroy's .45. Elroy said, "Drop the gun or I drop you."

Bill slowly let the gun slide to the ground and raised his hands. I walked toward him with my gun pointed at him and told him to turn around and put his hands against the cabin.

He complied and I searched him finding a knife but no guns. I cuffed him and showed him the warrant for his arrest. He asked, "How the hell did you find me?"

I told him it wasn't much of a problem. We took the shotgun, locked his truck and the cabin, and put the keys in his pocket.

Walking out to the road, we found a county sheriff sitting in his car, talking on the radio. It was no big surprise. He got out and asked us for our identification. Then he said, "I take it there were no problems."

I told him there were none and he got back into his car and drove away.

Elroy put our man in the back seat cuffing his hands to a ring that was chained to the floor. This allowed him to sit back with his hands between his knees. Elroy sat in the back with him.

We headed south toward Duluth and Highway 35 toward home. We stopped once for a bathroom break and burgers that we ate in the car.

When we got back to St. Paul, we walked our man into the downtown police station and gave our papers to the desk man.

Next, Stan called the Bondsman and told him the wanted man was in the city jail and he would be in to pick up the check in the morning. The Bondsman was one happy man! Six hundred for us was much nicer than the thousands he would have lost had we not gotten him.

It was about eight on a Friday evening. The man I was watching was parked in his usual spot.

He was in a black Buick in the North West comer of Rice Street and University Avenue. He liked that spot because he had a good view in all four directions. Also the White Castle across Rice Street provided food or drink if needed.

I had been watching him for about two weeks now from my parking spot just to the north of him where it was hard for him to see me.

I also knew he had runners out selling drugs about two or three miles west of here on the comer of University and Snelling Avenues . . .

They would call him on the cell phone if they needed more drugs or had a problem. Problems were taken care of with the .357 magnum I knew he had under the seat . . .

I know all this being a retired police officer. Yes, me, Elroy Sutton worked these streets here in St. Paul for over 25 years.

My partner, Stan Rutkowski and I worked our way up from street patrol to detectives going through robbery, homicide, and drug divisions.

The criminals I hated most were the drug pushers. They destroyed a lot of lives, including mine when they killed my only son, Buddy.

That is why I am here now watching his drug peddling bastard. The thought of Buddy made me choke back tears. I screwed the silencer on my .45 and tucked it into the pocket of my old camo jacket as I got out of my car.

His head turned toward me as I crossed the street walking toward him. I had my hat pulled down and looked like a shabby street person shuffling along.

I approached the driver's door and tapped on the partly open window. He lowered the window and said, "What you want, old man?"

I reached into my pocket and showed him $20 with my left hand while pulling my .45 out with my right and holding it against my leg, out of his sight. I said, "Whatever this will buy me."

He turned and reached into a bag in the back seat and pulled out a small plastic packet. When he turned back toward me, he was looking down the barrel of my .45.

He said, "Mother Fu—," as my first shot cut him off. I shot him again as he slumped over. I said, "That was for my Buddy."

I checked around to see if anyone had noticed anything but all was clear. I went through his pockets and found a big roll of cash. I left his drugs and handgun in the car, knowing the cops would take care of them.

I wanted it to look like a drug robbery gone bad; I guess that's what it actually was.

I got into my car and drove down University Avenue to a Burger King and called the police. I told them where to find a body and a lot of drugs. I knew a squad car would be there in minutes. I headed home with thoughts of my Buddy.

CHAPTER 4

I always liked to exercise and half-assed stayed in shape. I had self-taught defense and karate in the military and still practiced it regularly. It had paid off on lots of occasions while I was a police officer.

After a workout, I had stopped in a bar I frequented for a couple cool ones. I carry my cash in a money clip and, for some reason, I had more of a roll than I usually carry. I got out my money clip to pay for a beer and could not help but notice 2 young guys taking a good look at my roll. The boys were real interested now and were talking quietly between them.

I stopped on the way out a few minutes later to use the men's room. The bartender, who I had known for years, came in behind me. He said, "They went out when you came in here. Think you can handle them?"

"I see you still read people real well. Yes, I can handle them and I promise I won't do any more than I have to. Might even be fun."

"Okay," he said and headed back behind the bar and I went to the parking lot. I had almost made it to my car when they walked up on me. One walked behind me and the other came in front of me. The one in front said, "Let's have that roll you're carrying or you're going to get hurt."

I had my right hand in my jacket pocket. I spun around fast pulling my hand up and caught the guy behind me under his nose with a vicious chop. There was a crunching noise and his head snapped back as he went down, spraying blood out of his broken nose. The one in front of me charged and tried to hit me with a roundhouse right. I grabbed his wrist, stepping in to my left, twisting his arm and tripped him to the ground. When he tried to get up, I let go of his arm and chopped him very hard at the base of his skull. Then I kicked him very hard near the bottom of the rib cage. I know I broke some ribs.

"Enough, enough," the one on the ground with the broken nose shouted! He was sitting against a car, trying to stop the blood by squeezing his nostrils together.

The Bartenders voice behind me said, "Stan, Stan, When are these punks going to learn? You want me to call the cops?"

"No," I said. "But I better never see these two again." I pulled back my jacket and showed them my .38. They got into an old pickup and left.

As I drove home the thought of someone trying to kill my Dr. Clark was driving me nuts. I got him on the phone the next morning and set up a meet at the Lounge.

We got settled in at the Lounge with our drinks in a corner booth. I told him, "Doc, I owe you my life and I am going to help you clear up the mess you are in . . . Now tell me everything that happened."

He said, "I had just pulled in the hospital parking ramp and was about to turn up to the next level when my windshield exploded and my right arm felt like it was on fire. There was the sound of continuous gun fire. "

I laid down on the seat and let the car roll until it hit the curb in front of the entry door. The shooting stopped and I sat up and saw my dash and the tops of the car seats were full of bullet holes. My car was a mess!"

He continued, "People started to appear and helped me out of my car. My arm was bleeding like crazy. They got me into a wheelchair and started pushing me into the hospital. I remember looking back at my car and seeing it riddled with holes and fluids running out from under it. They got me to the emergency room where they patched me up."

I asked, "Doc, did you see anyone who was shooting at you?"

"No," he replied. "The police said they were shooting down from the open balcony one floor up."

"They, you just said they. How was it determined there was more than one shooter?"

Doc replied, "Because shell casings were found in two separate places. They recovered 40 shell casings. They were .223 casings leading the police to believe they were armed with M-16 rifles."

"Doc," I asked, "Can you think of anyone who wants you dead?"

"Well," he replied, "I believe it might be connected to a woman I lost on the operating table. I really didn't want to operate, but she would have died much sooner without the operation. Her son was adamant about her having the operation. I explained he risk to her and her son. They were insisting I go ahead, risks or no risks. So I did. After I lost her, I went to the waiting room to inform her son. He was in the company of several young black males. When he heard me say she had died, he completely lost it."

He screamed, "You son of a bitch, you were supposed to be the best!" "I approached him to try to calm him down and 2 of his companions grabbed me. One of them said, "You are a dead man, Doc."

Then some attendants came in and broke it up. As they were leaving, I heard one of them say to the son, "Slick, we take care of this later." As they were leaving, her son kept up his swearing tirade directed toward me.

"That's about it, Stan," he said as he motioned to the bartender for another round of drinks.

Then, remembering something, he added," Oh yeah, Stan, when the police interviewed me in the hospital, I learned who Slick was. He is a big time drug dealer in the Minneapolis and St. Paul area. The police have been after him for a long time. They said he is very careful and has the best legal help money can buy. He is also, a suspect in several gang killings. They warned me he is sure to try again. They suggested I go away or if I couldn't, to hire some protection. That's when I thought of you. I told the cops I would try to hire you and they said you were one of the best. So will you take the job?"

"Yes, I will." I replied.

"When can you start?" he asked.

"Thirty minutes ago." We made some arrangements and he left. He had agreed to stay in a hotel and not at home until he heard from me.

I called Elroy because I would be needing help. But it was Friday and no answer, as usual. I had no idea what was with Elroy on Fridays but I could never get hold of him on Friday's.

When I got home, there was a message on the machine to call Stan. Being as late as it was, I decided to call him in the morning. Stan was a great guy and I would have never made through my boy Buddy's death without him. I wondered what he would think if he found out what I was doing on Friday nights. Part of me thought he would understand.

About 9:00 the next morning, I called Stan. He told me he had talked to his Dr. Pal and needed my help to give his friend protection and find the man trying to kill him.

We met at the lounge to make our strategy plan for protecting the Dr. Also, it was Saturday and we had to figure our strategy for the horse track.

We settled in a booth and made out a schedule to keep an eye on the Dr.

Weekdays, Stan would pick him up at his hotel and stay near him until he took him back to his hotel at the end of his work day. Then he was mine, if he went out, until he returned to his hotel for the night.

The weekends, we split. I took Sundays and Stan, Saturdays. But this weekend the Dr. was out of town and would return on Monday.

So we figured to hit the racetrack and proceeded to plan the day's betting action. But tradition comes first. Stan called Cat over for his usual horse racing fact of the week . . . "Cat," Stan said. "Do you know the horse that paid the lowest odds after winning the Preakness?"

Cat replied, "Hell no!"

Stan said loudly, "Citation paid eleven for ten bet." The largest paid winner was a horse named Master Derby in 1975 after he beat the favorite, Foolish Pleasure. He paid twenty three to one."

Cat simply walked away shaking his head. There were a few chuckles from some of the bar patrons. One of them asked Stan, "How come horses are all two year olds or three year olds? Aren't some of them two and a half or even two and eight months?"

Stan replied, "Most racehorse foals are born between February 151 and April 30th.

The trick is to mate the mares at the right time so the babies are born as close as possible to the beginning of the year, making them as old as possible in the year they are born. However, if they are born in December instead of January, they are officially one year older when they are actually a day or two old."

CHAPTER 5

Stan, like most serious handicappers, always watched for trends at the track. What post positions won the most races, what trainers were doing well, and jockey records as well.

A trend he had noticed was a particular jockey and trainer match-up that was doing very well.

The trainer was McLean Robertson who had a very good win record at Canterbury. The jockey was Derick Bell. When Bell rode a Robertson horse, they had a great win percentage.

On one particular day, August 11th, this duo was entered in the 5th, 6th, 7th and 8th races.

Stan wasn't the only better who had noticed this combo so the odds stayed low, but you had to use them in any exotic bet.

Well, they won the 5th and my win bet paid $3.40. They won the 6th and my exacta paid $8.40. They won the 5th and the exacta paid Stan $6.70 and my trifecta paid a wonderful $41.80.

They did not win the 8th and I lost a $20.00 bet, but I finished with a great day. Once again, knowledge, not luck, paid off at the betting window because this pair had a 75% win day. And we had a great day, thanks to them.

We headed for the Lounge for a little party time with our winnings.

Sunday is my big exercise day. When Buddy was alive, we would walk together every Sunday, sometimes for several miles.

Stan and I had a good day at the track yesterday and had followed it up with a few drinks and a great meal at Mancini's Steak House on west 7th in St. Paul. Nick, the owner, was a kind and generous man-a legend in St. Paul. When he died, his funeral was a huge event.

After breakfast, I drove over to Long Lake Park. It's a park with great walking trails that go through wooded areas and around a small lake. I come here as often as I can for my exercise.

One of the trails starts with a walking bridge over a small stream. From the bridge you can see where the stream runs down into the lake. The other way, the stream runs under an old wood railroad bridge. The blackened timbers make it appear very old and rustic.

On this particular day, the weather was great. As I crossed the bridge, I could hear the bubbling sound of the water as it passed over and through the rocks below me.

As I started to leave the walking bridge, I heard what sounded like someone crying. It was coming from the upstream side toward the railroad bridge.

I looked through the metal framework on the side of the bridge and saw her. She was sitting on the stream bank between the wood support posts holding up the railroad bridge. She had her head resting on her arms that were crossed over her knees.

She was, I would guess, 15 or 16. Her hair was blond and cut short. Although she was about 20 yards away, I could see she was very attractive. As I watched her, she would raise her head and shake it back and forth as if in disbelief of what caused this heartbreak.

She couldn't see me because of the metal framework I was peering through. I was captivated by the scene. The babbling stream, sunlight filtering down through the thick tree foliage and the soft crying of the pretty young girl. I wanted to go to her, comfort her, and tell her everything was going to be alright. But I knew a strange man appearing out of nowhere would only cause her greater distress. I quietly walked away, leaving the beauty of it all. The girl didn't know it, but she had unknowingly given me a few moments of life's beauty and tragedy. I wished her well.

CHAPTER 6

That night I couldn't help but think of my boy, Buddy. I guess it was the scene in the park that brought it on.

I decided to go out and look for some dug selling action and the location of the man running it. It's easy to spot if you're an old retired cop and know what to look for.

Single guys who hang out on busy street comers or bus stops, who approach people or cars that are stopped for a light change. Guys who, sooner or later, head for a central location where the boss sits to resupply them or handle any problem.

That's the guy I want.

Being a Sunday night, I found only a few runners near the bus station and business was so slow, I gave it up early and headed home. Tomorrow would be the start for Stan and I to watch over his Dr. Pal.

Covering the good Dr. put a crimp in our betting schedule, so we changed our meetings to Friday nights after the good Dr. returned to his hotel for the night.

My weekend watch day was Sunday so I was to go make our bets on Saturday when Stan was watching the Doc.

The first week of watching the Doc was pretty quiet. We saw no one watching the hospital or his hotel. It was Friday night so I headed for the Lounge after the Dr. was in his hotel for the night.

Stan was sitting in his usual spot but must have just arrived because there was no glass in front of him. Cat was coming down toward him when I sat down. Stan, true to form, was about to lay a horse racing fact on him.

"Cat," Stan said, "Do you know the name of the first horse to win a million dollars?"

"No," Cat replied, "But I'm sure I am about to, so lay it on me."

"It was Citation in 1951 when he won the Hollywood Gold Cup," Stan said.

"Too bad he isn't around today. He must have been a great horse," Cat said as he laid a ten on the bar. "Now you two put your heads together and pick me a winner."

About an hour or so later, we picked up our paperwork and headed for the track. This was the weekend of the Breeder's Cup races being run at Monmouth Park. We had picked Indian Blessing, a Bob Baffert-trained entry, to win the Juvenile Fillies race. He was 3 to 1 in the morning line. He did win and paid $5.40.

In the next race, we picked Tale of Ekati at 7 to 2. He lost to a Nick Zitto entry, War Pass. A long shot, Lakuwood, beat us in the next race. Things were not looking good when we made a comeback in the 7th with a win by Midnight Lute, another Bob Baffert horse, paying $7.00.

Then we hit a good one in the 8th with Kip Deville. He was 6 to 1 in the morning line and paid $18.40—our best bet so far. The next race was the $2,000,000 Distaff. We bet a Robert Frankel horse named Ginger Punch. This was the race we put Cat's $10 bucks on. She won it and paid $11.00 giving Cat over fifty bucks. Cat was going to be one happy man.

The last two races were the $3,000,000 Turf and the big $5,000,000 Classic. Stan and I had not been able to agree on the same horse to bet on in the Turf. I made his bet for him on the favorite, Dylan Thomas. I took English Channel, a Todd Pletcher entry. English Channel won it paying $8.00.

The final race was the Classic and had an outstanding field of thoroughbred horses. Our money went on a great horse named Street Sense.

It was a classic horse race! Our horse lost to Curlin. I'm sure that race will go down in the annals of Horse racing history.

It had been a great day at the track! I had watched the best race horses. I'd won a few and lost a few plus had a great day's entertainment.

I got to the lounge and paid off Cat. He was one happy man! I asked if Stan had been in and he said no. I had a couple of beers and finally decided to give Stan a call.

He answered and, to my surprise, told me he was in the Washington County Jail. He told me he would be at the Lounge in an hour and explain what had occurred. He apparently couldn't talk at the time. Sometime later Stan came into the Lounge and said to me, "Come outside. I got something to show you."

The driver's side door had two holes in it. Bullet holes. Also the right side of the rear window had a large hole in it and the right side window was almost all blown out.

The rear windows were the result of a shotgun blast. The other holes were from a handgun.

Sand told me he and Dr. Clark had just left a club in Stillwater where the Dr. had attended a dinner. They headed west on Hwy 36 when a black SUV started to pass them on the left. There was a loud boom and shattered glass flew all over the inside of the car.

Stan hit the brakes just as more shots hit the side window and the dash as he cut to the right. As luck would have it, the ramp up to Hwy 5 was almost by him. Stan cut the wheel hard to the right again, going up the steep grassy incline to the top of the ramp. When he got to pavement on the ramp, he floored it, cutting left and crossing the bridge of Hwy 35. He then took the down ramp, headed back to Stillwater.

He asked the Dr. if he was okay. From the floor where he was curled up, Doc answered that he was. They didn't see the black SUV again.

They pulled into the Sheriff's station and were met by several officers. After a lot of explaining and paper work, they were allowed to leave. One of the officers took the Dr. home in a police car and Stan headed for the Lounge.

They had been very lucky. If Stan had not braked at the exact right time, the side window shots would have hit him for sure.

The next day was my day to watch the Dr., but he called in the morning and said, "I'm too shook up to go anywhere today, so you won't be needed. If I do go out, I will call you." I told him I understood and Stan would see him in the morning.

I thought about our situation all day. We were like sitting ducks for these crazies!

I figured, let's change the game. Time for me and Stan to take the offensive.

I spent a lot of time that day finding out all I could about this drug dealer named Slick. I checked the police record, talked discreetly, and got his address and where he liked to hang out.

I started to put a plan together as to where and when he would be the most vulnerable. This was one dangerous man, so I spent as much time as necessary to set this one up. This had no longer become for the Dr. This was for my Buddy. This dope peddling bastard was going down!

In 3 days I knew more about Slick than I think Slick knew about himself. He lived with his mother on Randolph Street and had lived there his entire life. He had graduated from the area's high school with good grades although in his senior year he had problems with the police and had been arrested 3 times on drug problems and assault but still graduated.

Most of his business was conducted out of another house he rented just off University Avenue on Victoria Street. His real name was Sylvester Stawl and he was now 24 years old. His arrest record was filled with mostly drug-related charges that never resulted in anything but overnight jail time. His legal defense attorney was one of the best. I'm sure he was extremely well-paid.

The week passed without incident when Stan called on Friday afternoon. He said another attempt was overdue. We agreed to meet at the Lounge Saturday morning because the Dr. wasn't going to leave the hotel all weekend.

I figured, good, then I could fill Stan in on what I had found out about our boy, Slick. I was sure Stan would agree it was time for us to go on the offensive.

CHAPTER 7

Stan came walking into the Lounge a few minutes after me. He took his usual stool next to me. Cat brought him his usual beer and couldn't wait to lay his usual horse racing fact on him.

Very loudly he said, "Cat, do you know the name of the jockey who had the most rides in the Kentucky Derby?"

Cat replied, "No, but I'm about to find out."

"Yes, you are," Stan said. "Bill Shoemaker had 26. Eddie Aracaro was second with 21."

"Well, who had the most wins?" Cat asked.

Stan replied, "Eddie Arcaro had 5 wins that ties him with Bill Hardtack.

Shoemaker won 4 times.

"OK," Cat said. "Now you pick me a winner today." He laid a ten on the bar in front of Stan as he turned to tend to another customer.

Stan took a call on his cell phone. When he closed it up, he said "Finish your beer; we got to roll. A guy in the doc's building told him he had seen a man do something to his car."

I downed the beer quick and we headed for the ramp where the Dr. parked his car.

Stan had told the Dr. not to go near the car.

We got there and it took only a few minutes to find it—an explosive device wired to the car's starter cable. We called the police and they got there with the Bomb Squad right behind.

Naturally, we had to go to the police station and fill out reports about the incident. When asked who we thought was behind this, we told them about Dr. Clark's history with Slick. They said they would bring in Slick for questioning.

We dropped the Dr. at his hotel and headed for the Lounge to pick up my car. On the way, Stan said, "You know we got damn lucky today. These bastards aren't going to quit until they get the Doc."

I said, "Stan, maybe we should go on the offensive."

"You mean like set them up some way?"

"Yeah, something like that. I'll work on it and see what I can come up with."

Stan said, "Yes, let me know. I agree we have to make some kind of move on this guy."

Little did he know my plan was to finish Slick, period—not just set him up! I continued to study Slick and followed him whenever I could. He had to have a vulnerable time in his daily routine.

I found it! It was Slick's lady. She lived in a building in St. Paul called Galtier Plaza. I'm sure old Slick was picking up the tab on the apartment. When he went to visit her or spend the night, his bodyguard would pull into the parking level of the building and drop off Slick. Slick would then walk to the elevators to go up to his little love nest. When he wanted to be picked up, the bodyguard would pick him up in the same place.

Now I wanted to find out which apartment his honey occupied. Also, I wanted to know if there was a regular schedule of when he visited the lady.

I caught a break one night while following Slick. He stopped at a flower shop but wasn't carrying any flowers then he came out. After he and the bodyguard left, I approached the counter clerk in the shop. I flashed my ID fast so the clerk couldn't really read it. I said "St Paul Police. Tell me where the man who just left wants his flower order delivered." She quickly looked down at the order and said, "Yes, Sir.—the Galtier Plaza" and gave me the room number. The flowers were to be delivered the next day.

My man, Slick, was in for a little surprise. I headed for the Galtier Plaza to check out the garage and the elevators. I also checked her room entrance and looked for any security cameras. I decided the best place to take him out was before he got to the elevators on the garage level. Friday night, I was parked near the elevators waiting.

About 8:00, old Slick arrived. He got out of the car and the bodyguard pulled away. I got out of my car as soon as the bodyguard left. I knew the security cameras were inside the glass doors leading to the room where the elevators were.

I had very little time to nail Slick before he got to those doors. He was 10-12 feet from the doors when I yelled, "Hey, Slick!" He stopped and turned toward me. Seeing the gun in my hand, he quickly turned and reached for the glass doors.

My shot hit him in the back of his head, spraying blood and tissue onto the glass doors. I put 2 more into his back as he started to fall. This caused him to fall forward against the door and it opened, allowing him to fall partly inside. I quickly got into my car and drove out onto 5th street. I figured the security guards, in their lobby office must have noticed Slick's body lying in the partly-opened doors on their camera screens.

I reached the corner of 5th and Sibley and was about to make a left turn to head back to the freeway when my luck appeared to run out. Two cops standing on the corner noticed me. One was an old friend of mine. His name was Jerry and we used to hang around a little over the years when I was on the force with him.

He had recognized me and yelled, "Hey, Elroy!" I stopped and rolled down the window. I replied, "Jerry! How you doing?"

They had both walked up to the car. Jerry said, "Oh, there was a problem in t he saloon up the street, but the shit head took off before we got there. How are things with you? Sorry to hear about your boy."

"Just fine," I replied.

Jerry turned to the other cop and said, 'This guy is an old retired cop. Believe it or not, he carried an old .45 as his piece for years and never got nailed for not carrying a regulation firearm. Not only did he carry it, he won departmental trophies with it."

I said, "Sorry, Jerry, but I'm running late and got to roll."

He asked, "Where you headed?"

I thought fast and said, "I got to meet Stan and I'm really late."

Jerry said, "You two still hanging out?" Turning to the other cop, he said, "Old Elroy and Stan were partners for years. Well, good to see you, Elroy. Take it slow and enjoy that retirement."

"You bet," I replied and drove away.

After I left, Jerry turned to his partner and said, "There goes one hell of a good cop! He retired after his son was shot by accident. A case of wrong place at the wrong time."

Then he added, "Say, Dick, did you notice a cordite smell coming from his car?"

"Damn!" his partner said. "So that's what I smelled. Well, maybe he was out shooting at the range somewhere."

"Yeah," Jerry replied. "That's probably it.

CHAPTER 8

"God damn the luck!" I said out loud and hoped like hell those 2 would forget they saw me. I figured by the time they got back in their squad car, the radio would be full of the shooting and the dead man in the Galtier building right next to them.

I decided I needed a drink, so I got off the freeway at Lexington Avenue and headed north about a mile to Katie's. It's a nice little bar and eating place with a friendly atmosphere and good food. I had known Katie for years. I had sandwich and 3 beers and headed for home. I was exhausted!

The next day, Saturday, I gave Stan a call. He said the Dr. wasn't going out until Sunday so we could meet as usual at the lounge and make our horse betting plans before we headed for the track.

I got there before Stan. Cat brought me my beer and asked if I heard about Slick getting shot. Cat knew about our problems with Slick.

I acted surprised and said, "No, what happened?"

"Someone shot and killed him in the Galtier Plaza parking level."

"This is great news, Cat. Do they know who did it?" I asked.

"I figured you would like that. No, I don't think they know who shot him."

I was on my second drink when Stan sauntered in. He laid out the Daily Racing Form as Cat brought his drink. Cat and I knew what was coming—the usual racing fact.

"Cat." Stan said loudly. "Did you know the horse racing record time for running the mile and a quarter that Secretariat set in 1973 of 1:54.9 still stands?"

"Damn," Cat replied sarcastically. "No, I didn't know that, Stan. Now pick me a winner today." He laid his usual $10 bill on the bar. He added, "By the way, Stan, I think your partner has some good news for you."

"Cat just told me Slick was killed last night," I said. "They got him in the basement parking level of the Galtier Plaza."

"That's great," Stan said. "I'm going to call the Dr. right now." He walked over to a quiet corner to use his cell phone. He returned a few minutes later and said, "What a relief. The Dr. is happy as hell. Someone did us a hell of a favor. I'll call the office tomorrow and get the scoop."

We then got down to work making our horse picks before heading out to Canterbury for some fun and relaxation. Just as we were about to leave, a fellow walked up to us and told us about his western boyhood and the cutting horses he rode. He told us about a fellow rancher who bred thoroughbred horses or claimed they were thoroughbred.

He asked Stan about how they find out if a horse is really a thoroughbred when he is bought or sold. Stan explained the whole thing in detail. The Jockey Club is the breed registry for thoroughbred horses in the United States, Canada and Puerto Rico. Their offices are in Lexington, Kentucky and New York City. Free tattoo identification service is provided by the agency. The tattoo is inside the lower lip and is best seen with a black light. Once a horse is registered, the name used must be available and cannot be used again for 17years. Names released for repeating are released annually in December. In use names or protected names can be found in the American Stud Book that is updated daily.

"By God, you're the man when it comes to horse information. I sure thank you," the man said.

We finally got to the track and it turned out to be a great day for me. I had a horse named Lord Frankenstein come in 3rd to win my trifecta bet at the Fairgrounds for a nice $416 bucks.

Of course, this required me to pick up the tab at any joint Stan picked. He wanted Italian so we ended up eating at one of his favorite spots, the Chanti Grill on Snelling Avenue. We both visited this place often because the food and service were always great!

The tab ran a little over $50 bucks but it ended a great day. It got even better when Stan told me he was picking up our paycheck from Dr. Clark the next morning.

CHAPTER 9

Stan dropped by the next morning. We settled up for my part of guarding the Dr. Then Stan asked me if I would be interested in going after another Bond Jumper. He claimed this one wasn't going to be too tough because it was a female.

She had been in charge of bookkeeping for a small company and had been brought up on theft charges. She had made bail but never showed for her court appearance.

Stan had checked her out and found she had a bad gambling habit. No doubt she wasn't doing well with it, thus the theft from her employer. Stan had talked with her coworkers and her landlord. They told him she truly loved gambling at the Turtle Lake Casino in Wisconsin.

We visited the casino the next afternoon. We sat down with their security staff and showed them our warrant and a picture of her Stan had acquired. She wasn't there.

The following Friday night about 7:00 Stan called. He had gotten a call from the casino. They had spotted our lady gambler.

Stan picked me up and we headed north on Hwy 35. In less than an hour, we walked into the Turtle Lake Casino. Our lady was pointed out to us sitting at a Black Jack table. For a few minutes, we observed her from behind. The dealer had a 6 card up (worst card there is for the dealer) and our lady had a pair of 9s and did not split them. The dealer hit his 6 twice and caught a face card, breaking his hand. Had the lady split her cards, she probably would have won both hands instead of one.

The casino security guard who had accompanied us to her table put his hand on her shoulder and told her, "These 2 gentlemen would like a word with you." She turned toward us and asked, "Who are you?" Before Stan or I could answer, the man seated next to her asked "Yeah, who in the hell are you?" He obviously had quite a bit to drink.

Stan said, "We have a warrant for our arrest," and started to pull her off her stool.

"Take your God Damned hands off her," her companion said as he pushed Stan back.

I grabbed his outstretched arm and snap-twisted it behind him while putting my other arm around his neck. That made him realize he was powerless to be any help to his lady friend.

"OK, OK, I don't want any trouble," he said. I released him and the security guard made him pick up his chips and led him away.

We took the lady to a quiet area where Stan showed her our papers on her. She accepted the fact her little run from justice was over. After cashing in her chips, we put her in the car. Not feeling the need to hook her up, I rode in the back with her. On the way home, she told us the sad tale of becoming addicted to gambling—an addiction that cost her a marriage to, in her words, "The greatest guy alive;" eventually, her job and finally, her freedom.

We turned her over to the proper authorities when we reached St. Paul. Then Stan called the Bondsman and made his day to have her secure in the lock-up.

Stan dropped me at home and I put in an hour or so on my computer working the various horse betting web sites. I was getting ready for our usual Saturday routine at the Lounge before hitting the horse track.

CHAPTER 10

I still hadn't heard any more about Slick and I wanted to find out if Stan had called our old Captain. What I really was wondering about is if they, in any way, were looking at me for a suspect. I wanted to be nonchalant about it. I didn't want Stan to start wondering if I had something to do with Slick's shooting.

So, due to Slick's elimination, it was back to our weekend routine. We got settled in at the Lounge in the morning and, as always, Stan had to lay a horse racing fact on our friend, Cat. When he brought us our drinks, Stan loudly said, "Cat, do you know only 3 fillies have won the Kentucky Derby?"

Cat, with his usual sarcasm, replied, "No, but I'm about to find out who they were, ain't I?"

"Yes, indeed," Stan said, "Regret in 1915, Genuine Risk in 1980, and Winning Colors in 1988.

Cat said, "That was just great, Stan. Now pick me a filly or something in today's races that will win me some money today." He then pulled out his roll and put a ten down in front of Stan.

It was opening weekend at the Oaklawn track in Arkansas. Oaklawn, being in the same time zone as we are, got the most part of our bets for today.

Oaklawn started with a cheap maiden race that was won by a 10-1 shot named Sneaky Chic. The second race was won by an unbelievable run by a 50-1 shot named Deputy Tice. The long shot day at Oaklawn continued and we lost Cat's ten in the 4th race on a horse named Rock N Sydney that placed.

The big race of the day was the 8th. A six furlong stakes race called the American Beauty. There was a duel entry that I liked, so I put $20 on one of them named Fast Deal. Fast Deal placed. I guess he wasn't properly named. The other duel entry ran dead last.

Finally came the last race of a terrible day for us. A four year old claiming race. We lost it too. A damn long shot named Sudden Sid won it paying 50 to 1.

We hit the second floor bar and pounded down a couple of quick ones before heading to the parking lot. The end of a bad day at the track.

Monday morning came and the nightmare started. About 10:00 there was a loud knocking on my door. I opened it and a lady and a tall man were there. They both flashed badges and asked if they could come in. I had them take a seat and asked what I could do for them.

The lady said, "I'm detective Taylor Labare and this is detective George Mason." I'd never met them before so I said, "Well, did you know I'm a retired officer?"

"Oh yes," detective Mason said, "We know all about your career. We have a few questions to ask you, but first we would like your handgun. I believe it's an old model 1911-.45 automatic." With that he handed me the legal paper to take my .45.

I acted shocked and asked, "What is this all about?" The lady detective Taylor said, "We work homicide and have reason to believe you might have been involved in a recent shooting."

"What shooting?" I asked.

"A man was killed in the parking garage of the Galtier Plaza," she replied. "It was someone you have had some problems with. This was a man you knew as Slick."

"Yes, I knew Slick but I didn't shoot him."

"Would you get us your .45?" Detective Mason asked. "We will run some tests on it and see if it was used in the shooting. Be assured if it wasn't used, you will get it back and probably never see us again."

I reluctantly got up and went to get my old .45. I noticed they both had their hands inside their coats when I came back into the room with my gun. I had the clip in my one hand and the gun in the other. I handed them both to the female detective. She worked the slide to be sure it was empty. They both got up to leave.

Her partner said, "Don't leave town," and they left.

My heart was racing so bad I had to sit down. "God Damn, it must have been those 2 cops," I said out loud as my mind was racing. Why hadn't I changed the barrel? on that damned gun? Why didn't I see this coming after Jerry and that other cop had seen me?

Then the phone rang. I answered and to my surprise it was Stan. He said, "I got a couple of phone calls about you being a suspect in Slick's death. Why don't I drop by and we will go out for a couple of drinks and talk?"

"Okay," I said.

About 20 minutes later I heard Stan's car horn, We rode up to Katie's bar about 2 miles from my house in the corner shopping center at Hwy 96 and Lexington.

We got our drinks and settled in a booth. Stan said, "You want to tell me about it? I didn't want to ask you about it over the phone. This being a murder investigation, your phone could be tapped."

My mind went to the short time I had left them in the living room to go get my gun. Maybe they did put a bug in my phone or plant some other device. I would check for something later.

I asked, "Stan, how did they get on me for this?"

Stan replied, "Here is what I have been told. People remember us guarding the Dr. and Slick's boys trying to take him out. It was easy for somebody to put two and two together. Plus, he was killed with a .45. Your reputation for carrying a .45 is known by every cop in the city."

"Did you hear anything about anybody who claims to have seen me at the scene?" I asked. "No," Stan answered, "Not that I've heard but I'm sure they didn't tell me everything." I thought to myself that it didn't look like Jerry or the other cop had ratted me out. If they had, I'd probably be in the lockup by now.

"You and I know these punks today don't carry .45's. They favor the 9mm or something smaller," Stan pointed out. Then his phone rang. He answered and a few minutes later he gave me a funny look.

He said to me, "You better have another drink. The lab report is in. The lab matched the slugs they took from Slick to your .45. They are processing the warrant for your arrest as we speak."

"Well," I said, "I guess it's time to call a lawyer."

"I'll do everything I can to help you, Leroy," Stan said. "I think I know what went down."

"Thanks," I replied. "Now take me home. I don't want to keep them waiting." Sure enough, when we pulled into my driveway, a black car pulled in behind us.

We got out and it was the same 2 detectives that had come to my house to pick up my .45. The lady detective approached drawing her weapon. She said, "Put your hands against the car. You are under arrest on suspicion of First Degree Murder."

I complied and she did a thorough job of patting me down. I wondered why her partner didn't do it. She cuffed me and put me in their car.

Stan said, "You didn't have to cuff him."

"Stay out of this," the other cop said, "This has nothing to do with you."

"Screw you," Stan replied, "He has more time as a cop than you 2 combined."

"Yeah, yeah," replied the cop, "Maybe this isn't the first time he screwed up. But, you being his old partner would know all about that, wouldn't you?"

"Why you arrogant prick," Stan shouted as he approached the 2 detectives, "How about I shut your God Damned mouth?"

The detectives both drew their guns and ordered Stan to halt. He complied.

The female ordered, "Both of you shut up!" To the other cop she said," And you get in that car NOW," He uttered something under his breath but complied.

"Elroy, I'll give Earl Cane a call," Stan said. Earl was a damn fine lawyer they both knew.

"You better get him a hell of a good lawyer. From what I see, he is going down for murder one," the male detective hollered from the car as it backed out.

Stan called Earl right away and told him of Elroy's plight. He agreed to defend him. He told Stan they would get him before a judge within 48 hours. Then bail would be set and a hearing date. Then Stan called the bail bondsman they had worked for and, thanks to their saving him thousands of dollars over the years, agreed to post bond for Elroy, up to a reasonable amount. What that amount was, he wouldn't say.

Two days later, Elroy was brought before a judge. A court date was set and bail was brought up. Earl pointed out he was a retired officer who had been wounded in the line of duty and decorated twice for service above and beyond. The judge set his bail at $100,000 and my bondsman stood up and said he would post bail.

About an hour later, Elroy was released. He walked out to my car and got in. Putting his hand on my shoulder, he said, "I can't thank you enough, Stan. I'll never forget it. I owe you man."

I know you would do the same for me," Stan said. "Now let's go have a drink and talk." We stopped at the Savoy and took a booth. We got our drinks and Stan said, "Okay, Elroy, I have made some discreet inquiries and all they have is your gun that does match up with the slugs in Slick."

I said, "Stan, have you heard anything about 2 cops coming forward with information about maybe seeing me in the area about the time of the shooting?"

"No," Stan said, "But I think you should tell me all about this."

So I told Stan about the cop Jerry and his partner talking to me near the Galtier Plaza building the night of the shooting.

Stan, who also knew Jerry said, "You want me to talk to Jerry?"

"No, let's let it ride. Maybe they forgot about it."

"Okay if that's the way you want to play it. We'll let it go for now."

Late the next day Stan called me. He said, "I've been checking around. Do you remember that cop with Jerry that night?"

"Yes," I said, "His name was Dick something."

"Well I don't think you have to worry about him. He quit and took a job in San Francisco. Some friend of his runs a detective agency out there and he joined up with him."

"Well, that is some good news. Now all I have to worry about is good old Jerry,"

I said, "Let's hope he is forgetful."

Stan said, "You know it still looks bad for you. That gun may end up putting you away."

"Well," I replied, "We will know pretty soon. Earl said the hearing date is next week."

CHAPTER 11

They judge had suspended my license to carry until after my trial. I felt naked without my old .45. I was needed to catch up on some gun repair work at the Sporting Goods Store where I worked, so I headed over there the next morning. I stashed an old .38 under my car seat. I figured I might get by because I wasn't actually carrying it on me.

I was in the shop at work when one of the counter clerks came into the shop. He said, "Elroy, there is a guy out here who wants to trade in a glock 17. You want to check it out?"

I said, "Sure, the 17 is like the 19 except it's made of polymer." I followed the clerk out and he introduced me to the man and he handed me the holstered glock.

I asked him, "Where did you get this?"

"Someone owed me some money and gave me the gun about a week ago," he replied, "Why do you ask?"

"Just not many ofthese17'saround," I said as I took it out of the holster. I then reached into the display case and got a glock 19 out. I handed them both to the man and said, "Feel the difference I weight?"

He replied, "Damn, mine weighs less than half as much as the 19."

"You're right," I said, "because it is made of Palomar. The only steel in the gun is the barrel and one small spring. They tried to make the 17 illegal back in the 80's because it could get by airport security if you removed the barrel."

"Hell," the man replied, ""You mean I can't trade or sell it?"

"No," I said, 'Now it is popular even in some city police departments. You can even buy them in some gun shops."

"Thanks for all the information. I believe I will hang onto it." He picked up the gun and left.

45

The clerk said, "Well, I'm glad you were here. I would have taken it for a model 19. It sure looked good."

I said, "Actually it could be the handgun of the future. Plastic is a lot cheaper than metal and it's just a question of time until they come up with plastic tough enough to be used as a barrel."

The day passed fast due to my being so far behind in my gun repair work. Finally 5:00 rolled around and I checked out and headed home.

That night after I finished supper, I got on the Daily Racing Form website and discovered the first betting window would be open this weekend to bet weeks ahead on the Kentucky Derby and Kentucky Oaks. They list the top 23 entrees and, for a weekend, you can bet to win on the Derby or the Oaks.

The odds that are listed are locked in so you can get some good bets. They also list a field bet. This bet covers all horses listed at the mutual field. One bet covers all the mutual entrees.

The first horse to win as a field bet in the Kentucky "Derby was Flying Ebony in the 1925 Derby. The field bet paid 7 to 1. The next mutual field winner was Count Turf in 1951 and he paid $31.20 to win. There are 3 windows open for betting on the 2 races.

If your horse drops out, you lose your bet. The final odds for each window are posted after each window closes.

This year's window 1 opened February 7th—10th. I will put $25 on War Pass to win the Derby and another $25.00 on Indian Blessing to win the Oaks, a race for 3 year old fillies.

In 2007 there was $520,688 bet on the Kentucky Derby that was won by Street Sense. Bets made in window 1 on Street Sense paid $22.80. Bets made in window 2 paid $18.20, and bets made in window 3 paid $15.40. Thus the benefit of betting during the open windows is obvious (providing you pick the winning horse).

The largest window I payoff was in 2003. That was the year Smarty Jones won the Derby. For a $2.00 bet, you won $188.00.

Stan and I drove out to the track Saturday afternoon. We made our window bets on the Kentucky Derby and the Oaks. The weather was terrible, even by Minnesota standards, so we made a few bets on some later races that we could watch on Cable TV.

CHAPTER 12

My morning started with a phone call from my lawyer, Earl. He informed me my preliminary hearing would be held in 10 days.

I asked him if anything new had been brought up. He said, "No, not that I know of. Their whole case is still that gun of yours and the matching slugs taken from Slick's body. Was there something else you were expecting?"

"No," I replied, "I was just wondering."

After Earl hung up, I called Stan and told him about my court hearing date.

The Preliminary Hearing determines if a person should be charged based on the evidence presented. The Prosecution must present enough evidence to prove probability of guilt. The Defendant offers anything that could explain why charges should not be brought. The case, if not dismissed, is forwarded to the proper court for trial.

I called Stan and told him the gun was their whole case.

Stan replied, "Well, it could be worse. At least nobody saw you."

Suddenly remembering my phone could be tapped, I said, "Saw me do what?"

Stan paused for a minute and must have realized the mistake he had just made and said, "I mean whoever is trying to set you up and lie about seeing you at the scene."

"Oh," I replied, "You're right. That would be hard for me to disprove. Living here alone and all, it would be tough for me to verify my whereabouts."

"That's true," Stan said, "You take it easy now and I'll see you Saturday morning at the Lounge as usual." I had to give Stan credit. He covered up his mistake pretty good.

Saturday morning we met as usual and as the old routine called for, Stan called Cat over for his weekly horse racing fact.

Loudly, Stan said, "Cat. Did you know the first American counter clockwise horse race was the 1921 Belmont? All previous races ran clockwise as they do in England."

"Great," Cat sarcastically replied, "Now that is something that will come up every day! I hope the horse you bet for me today knows which way to run."

That got a big laugh from all the bar patrons!

There were 2 big races scheduled for today. The first was at Laurel Park. A 7 furlong on the dirt called the Barbera Fritchie Handicap. The race was for a $300,000 purse.

The favorite was a horse named Control System. She had a great Bayer speed rating her last time out running 6 furlongs with a 106. She also won the race before that with a Bayer rating of 98.

However, the horse I really liked was the number 3 entry, Golden Dawn. She ran a fantastic race her last time out, a 6 furlong race she won by 6 lengths with a Bayer rating of 97.

The second big money race of the day was at Tampa Bay Downs. The Sam Davis, a mile and a sixteenth with a purse of $200,000. The favorite in this one was a horse named Z-Humor, a 3year old colt. He had won his last race going a mile and one eighth by a neck. His Bayer rating was 96.

Stan had convinced Cat to make an exacta bet for a change with his ten bucks on the race at Laurel Park. Stan bet Cat's $10 on a $5 exacta box bet on number 4, Golden Dawn and the favorite number 9, Control System.

That looked good to me, so I made the same bet myself. Also in the big race at Tampa, I put a twenty on a horse named Fierce Wind. Fierce Wind had won his last race going a mile and one eighth, leading all the way and finishing with a Bayer rating of 89.

We, including Cat, had a great day at the track. In the Laurel race, Fierce Wind won, giving me a nice payday of $88.00.

At Laurel Park, Cat's Golden Dawn finished first at 5 to 1 and the favorite Control System placed. Cat won his exacta paying him $67.00. We didn't win all of our bets but finished well ahead. We headed for the Lounge to make Cat's day. On the way, we discussed my upcoming hearing. Stan said, "Well, you never know for sure what just might happen." When I asked what he meant by that, all he would say is, "Things have a way of turning out a little different sometimes."

The morning of the hearing, Stan and I were standing near the entrance to the courtroom. The Assistant District Attorney who was handling the state's case was standing near us going over some papers with 2 other people.

Suddenly Jerry, the cop I had been so concerned about, bumped into me, nearly pushing me into the Attorney. "So sorry," he said. Then, quite loudly, he said, "Hey, it's you, Elroy. I haven't seen you since you retired. How in the Hell are things going?"

When he said this, he looked me right in the eyes and Stan, next to me, nudged me with his elbow. It took me a second to react to what had just occurred. Then I said, "Not too well. I'm about to enter a hearing to answer a charge of murder one."

Jerry replied, "Sorry to hear that. I wish you the best of luck, pal. It must be all a mistake."

We then started to enter the courtroom, Stan quietly said, "Must be another one of those that appears different things." I looked at him and he gave me a wink. I knew he had set up the whole thing with Jerry to have the D.A. overhear Jerry say he hadn't seen me since I retired. I began to wonder if Stan had any more surprises for me.

I sat up front next to Earl at the defense table as the proceedings started. The evidence of the gun was enough to bring a murder charge in the first degree against me.

A trial date was set and I was taken into custody. Earl asked what bail there would be and the judge set it at $150,000. Our bail bondsman said he would put up the bail, and I was to be released in the morning.

I decided I would enjoy life to its fullest for the 2 weeks I had before the start of my trial. That's what I told Stan the next morning when he picked me up.

Stan said, "Just be damn careful. You're in enough trouble without getting your bail revoked by making a stupid mistake."

"Well," I replied, "I'm going to have a great time anyway because it sure looks like my ass is headed for jail"

Stan replied, "Earl, remember what I said about things turning out different than you thought they would."

"What the hell can change? They got me dead to rights."

"We will see, we will see," Earl said.

The next 2 weeks, I had a ball. I started by calling a lady acquaintance of mine that I had occasionally dated. I wined and dined her at Axel's on Cleveland Avenue.

Then we headed for Minneapolis and the Blue Star Room on ninth.

We both liked jazz, so the next few nights we hit all the good spots. The Dakota Club on the Nicollet Mall, The Bar Lureat, Cafe Luxx, and the Artists Quarter back in St. Paul. My bank account took one hell of a beating but the good times rolled.

Not only that, but the lady friend and I developed a nice relationship. I told her of my horseracing hobby and she seemed very interested. So I invited her to go out to the track.

The big races for the weekend were a grade one Golfstream Park Turf stakes race and the Fountain of Youth. Dawn wanted me to teach her the basics of betting the horses. Her interest seemed genuine and she proved to be a quick learner. I told her the basics to look for such as the jockey and trainers win percentages. Also the times the horses had run the distances in and the times between races the horses were to run; how they had placed in their last few times out. Also, if the purses were smaller or bigger they were running for.

I also told her to check and see if the horse was being shipped in for the race because it cost money to ship a horse. The owner and trainer must think the horse has a chance to win if it's shipped in.

When we got to the track, she was very excited. She had never been there and was anxious to try out what I had taught her about handicapping horses. We picked up a Daily Racing Form and I showed Dawn how to translate all the symbols and jargon.

I had called Stan to see if he wanted to go along, but he said, no, that something had come up he needed to take care of. He didn't explain what it was. Sounded mysterious to me.

We had a blast at the track! We won some and lost some, but Dawn never lost her enthusiasm. We finished the day about $40 ahead.

It had been a great day and we decided to have a dinner of spaghetti and meatballs at home. That was the first night Dawn spent the night with me. I began to realize my life could be changing. The trouble was, I could lose it all at trial. I just could not tell Dawn if the charges were real.

CHAPTER 13

Stand sat and watched the 2 men go by him for the 3rd time. They were in an older, dark colored Caddy. They would stop or slow down when going by the bus stops.

Openly they would offer drugs to the people in or near the bus stops and shelters. This practice was so common that users knew they just had to hang around a bus stop to score whatever they needed.

Stan had been watching this same car for several nights and had plans for it. But for the plan to work and getting the charges against his pal, Elroy, dropped, he had to have another person's help.

A few minutes later, his cell phone rang. He answered and said he would meet the caller. About 10 minutes later, he pulled into an old abandoned railroad parking lot off Pennsylvania Avenue.

There was a car parked in the back of the lot with one man in it. Stan pulled up to the driver's side. The man rolled down his window and handed Stan a paper bag. He said, "This better go as planned or we go to jail and kiss our pensions goodbye."

"Don't worry," Stan replied, "I'll see you Saturday night." They then left the parking lot going in different directions—Stan heading back to University Avenue and the other toward downtown.

After Dawn left for work the next morning, I got a chance to read the paper. I saw where 2 men, suspected of selling drugs, were shot to death in their Cadillac near a bus stop on University Avenue. Drugs were found in the car. Thoughts of Buddy rushed into my head. I was happy to hear they were shot but kind of glad it wasn't me who killed the swine.

I guess Dawn was changing me and I kind of liked the change. Kissing someone goodbye in the morning when they left for work was kind of nice.

I didn't hear from Stan again until Thursday afternoon. He asked how things were going and how I had done at the track. He also asked if I had heard from my lawyer, Earl. I told him no, not since the hearing.

About an hour later, Earl did call. To my surprise he informed me we were going to appear before a District Judge at 10:00 the next morning. I was shocked!

I asked Earl what the hell was going on? He said, "I have asked for a special hearing to dismiss all charges. I have new documented evidence they will be shocked to see. I can now prove your gun couldn't have been used in the shooting you are accused of. See you at 10:00 at the courthouse."

I wanted to call Stan but remember red my phone might be tapped so I decided to use my cell phone and call from the car. He answered and I told him the good news. For some reason, he really didn't seem all that surprised. He said he would meet me at the hearing and added, "Remember what I've been saying about things appearing different sometimes."

That night I told Dawn what had happened and she said, "There. I knew they had to be wrong. I will try to get the day off for the hearing."

I got to the hearing room a little early and took my seat next to Earl at the front table. I didn't see Dawn but did give Stan a wave in the rear seats. Present at the other table were the District Attorney and several other men. They didn't look happy.

The Judge entered the room and took his seat telling everyone to be seated. He then informed the room that were it not that the accused was a decorated police officer, this hearing would not be taking place. He then instructed Earl to proceed and present his new evidence.

Earl stood up and said, "Your Honor, my defendant Elroy Sutton has been wrongfully charged with murder in the first degree. The District Attorney claims he did it because ballistics tests he had taken show my client's gun was the murder weapon, or so he claims they do. Actually they don't."

The District Attorney jumped up and said, "Your Honor, we have not seen any documented evidence proving this man not guilty as charged!"

The Judge said, "Sir, please sit down. We will let the defense finish. Then you will have your chance to speak."

Earl then picked up some papers and walked over to the District Attorney's table and handed him several. Then he handed the rest to the court attendant who gave them to the Judge.

Earl said, "Your Honor, last Saturday evening 2 men were shot and killed on University Avenue here in St. Paul. I would like to add these individuals were drug dealers with prior convictions. Proof of this is now on your desks along with a copy of the police report and their arrest records. Yes, drug dealers. Just like the one my client is accused of killing," he added with zest. "The bullets taken from their bodies were .45 caliber. Ballistic tests done by the State Crime Lab show they were fired from the same gun my client is accused of using in his murder charge."

The District Attorney interrupted saying, "Your Honor. My office wasn't aware such tests were being taken. We want time to verify these tests to be authentic."

The Judge said, "You will get your chance to speak. Now, no more interruptions from you. Is that understood?"

"Yes, Your Honor," the attorney replied and took his seat. The Judge turned to Earl and said, "Continue, Earl."

"Yes, Your Honor. I now wish to call someone up to verify these ballistics tests were taken by the State Crime Lab." Earl then turned and motioned a man to come forward to the bench and had him show his credentials proving he was a State Crime Lab employee.

Earl then asked the judge that the man be sworn in. The judge had the man sworn in after seating him in the witness chair.

"Now," Earl said as he walked toward the man. "Did you do the tests on the slugs in question?"

"Yes," the man replied. He then read off the serial number of the gun that was tested. Earl asked, "Did the slugs match the markings of the .45 the police have under lock and key?"

"As near a perfect match as you can get," he replied.

"So you're saying a gun under lock and key with solid security was used in a killing Saturday?" Earl asked.

"What I'm saying is a gun, either that one or one like it, was used in this shooting," he answered.

"Earl asked, "Is it possible 2 guns can leave the same markings?"

"Very rare," the man answered. "In my 15 years of experience, I've seen it happen only once."

"Thank you," Earl said to the crime lab tech.

Earl then addressed the Judge. "Your Honor, we believe the charges against my client should be dropped. We have just proven my client's gun was not used in the shooting the District Attorney has accused him of."

"Thank you, Earl," the Jude replied. "Now I will hear what the District Attorney has to say."

The Assistant District Attorney stood up and said, "Your Honor, this is the firs we have heard of this. We would like some time to verify these things. First off, we would like to know who authorized the release of this gun for the additional tests on this recent shooting."

Earl jumped up, "It was the watch commander as the log in front of you shows."

"Why would he do such a thing without contacting my office first," the now upset Assistant District Attorney asked.

Earl replied, "To save a decorated retired police officer with a distinguished service record from being convicted of a crime he didn't commit."

The Judge said, "Gentlemen, sit down, now. I have heard enough. I am releasing Elroy Sutton. I am satisfied he was wrongfully charged with this crime. I order charges to be dropped. Mr. Sutton, you are free to go."

"But, Your Honor, we need time to go over all of this," the Assistant District Attorney pleaded. "No," the Judge said, "It has been proven the gun, in secure police custody, could not have been used. Therefore, all charges have been dropped." With that the Judge got up and left the courtroom.

Dawn, who had entered the courtroom after proceedings had started, shouted out, "Yes, Yes," as she started to run down the aisle to the defendants table where she gave Elroy and Earl each a big hug.

Stan shook Elroy's hand and said, "Congratulations! Now you know what I meant when I said things can appear differently."

"Wow, they sure can. Thanks a million, Stan." a smiling Elroy replied. Then, turning to Earl, he shook his hand and thanked him for a job well done.

"Glad we could clear it up before an actual trial," Earl replied, "The bill will be in the mail," he added with a big smile. "Now go celebrate and stay out of trouble."

CHAPTER 14

We headed for the door. Dawn was hanging on to me like she would never let me go. I felt like one lucky man.

I could only guess at what must have occurred, but I knew Stan had pulled it off somehow and we would talk later. We stopped for drinks and had some lunch. Stan said we would get together later and left. Dawn and I headed for my place. In the car, she surprised me. She said, "We are going to sit down when we reach your place and you are going to tell me the real story."

I said, "I can never do that because some other people are involved who could lose everything if certain facts about this whole thing became known."

"You mean Stan?" Dawn asked.

I replied, "Yes, and maybe not just him."

She sat quietly for a while. Finally she turned to me and said, "Elroy, take me home. I need some time to think about this."

"What do you mean, think about this? Do you mean you and I?" I asked.

She replied, "Suddenly I think I finally realize things are not what I thought they were."

She didn't say anything else until we got to her place. Then she turned to me and said, "I'm going to need some time. I'll call you in a few days." She had tears in her eyes.

His old and trusted friends was working there while waiting for his retirement papers.

Stan had saved his life a few years back, so it was like he was settling an old debt. Stan told me to forget about him and forget his name.

After we had picked up my gun and were driving down Kellogg, Stan took a right onto the Wabasha Bridge over the Mississippi River. He stopped in the middle of the bridge and said to me, "Elroy, give me that damned gun."

He was dead serious. Because he had just saved my ass from going to jail, I felt I had no choice so I handed it to him. He threw it out the car window into the river. Then he said, "There, now it is over."

"Okay, I guess it is and I owe you big time, Stan," I replied.

Stan said, "Let's not talk about it again. No more shootings, Elroy. This is the end."

"I give you my word, Stan. No more shootings."

We got to the Lounge and Stan and 1 sat in our usual spots. Cat brought us our usual and we tried to relax after another tough day. But every bar has its characters.

Either they are loud and obnoxious or experts in some strange field. The Lounge had a poet and a comedian and both were in attendance. The joke teller happened to hear me tell Cat my case had been dismissed and 1 was not going to jail. He stood up and clapped his hands to get the bar's attention.

He loudly said, "Have you fellows heard about the 3 prisoners about to be executed?"

Cat, with his usual sarcasm, said, "No, but we are about to."

The joker continued, "The Warden asked each man in turn what they wanted for their last meal"

"Lasagna," replied the first prisoner. He ate his plate of lasagna and was then led to the execution chamber.

"I'd like Lobster," the second prisoner said. The Warden complied and when he finished eating, he was also taken to the execution chamber.

The third prisoner said, "I request a big bowl of fresh strawberries topped with whipped cream."

"Sorry," the Warden said. "Strawberries are out of season."

"Oh, that's okay," replied the prisoner, "I'll wait."

It got a good laugh, even a chuckle from Cat. The guy had a reputation for being a comic and loved being in the limelight.

Not to be outdone, the bar poet stood up and loudly said, "Gentlemen, if I may."

This guy was very well known in the local bars, so all went quiet.

"Rush headlong and hard into life,

Or just sit at home and wait.

All things good, and all the wrong will come right to you, it's fate.

Hear the music, dance if you can.

Dress in rags or wear your jewels.
Drink your choice, nurse your fears.
In this honkeytonk of fools."

With that, he lowered his hands and head in a bowing gesture. He received applause and shouts from the bar patrons.

Stan turned to me and said, "I would like to follow that guy around and record some of that stuff."

"Yes, "I said, "And you rarely hear him repeat one on anyone night."

We then settled down to business with the Daily Racing Form. But before we really got into it, Stan turned to me and asked, "How are things with you and Dawn going?"

"She told me she needs to think about things after my legal problem got settled.

She wanted me to tell her the whole true story. I told her I could never do that because it would implicate other people."

"You damned right you can't," Stan said. "Like we said, the truth gets buried with us."

"I know, Stan, I know," I replied.

CHAPTER 15

There were 4 big races that we concentrated on for the day. One at Golfstream Park called the Golfstream Handicap, a one and 3/16th race on dirt. They were running for a purse of $350,000 with a small field of 5 entries, but they were 5 very good horses, evenly matched.

The one factor that stood out at me was the distance. A mile and 3/16th is a long way to run, even for thoroughbreds. The longest odds in the morning line were 6-1. A tough race to handicap.

To make it even tougher, one entry was 8 to 5, and another was 2 to 1. With this short field of 5, these two would have to be used in any combination or exacta bet. I finally decided to go with a single win bet. I will put $20 on the 8 to 5 entry—a horse named Fairbanks.

The next big races were at Santa Anita. Three races in all including the 7th that was the Sham. The Sham is considered a big prep race for the Kentucky Derby. There were 7 entries in the sham, but one, Coast Guard, scratched. The favorites were Colonel John at 9 to 5, and El Gato Molo at even odds. El Gato Molo was being ridden by one of my favorite jockeys, Flores.

One other horse I liked was number 7, Perfect Times. I decided in this race to bet a $2.000 Trifecta Box on horse #1, El Gato Molo with #6, Colonel John and #7, Perfect Times.

The 8th race at Santa Anita was the Kilroe Mile on the turf. The purse was $300,000 with 7 entries. The favorite was War Monger at 8 to 5 . . . I liked the number 4 horse, Artiste Royal and decided to put $20 on him to win and $40 to place.

The 9th race at Santa Anita was the race of the day for all handicappers, the Million Dollar Santa Anita Handicap, 1 ¼ miles on dirt.

Another part of the handicapper's challenge was the big field. Fourteen horses were entered and 3 of the top trainers had horses entered in the race, Bob Baffert, Doug O'Neal, and Robert Frankel.

We called Cat over and told him this was the race for his $10.00 bet; and, of course, Stan had to lay another horse racing fact on him. He asked Cat, "What horse ran the slowest Kentucky Derby time in history?" Cat replied, "How the hell would I know?"

Stan said, "A good handicapper knows these things, Cat. The horse was Stone Street. He ran the 11f4 mile Derby in 2:15.20 in 1908."

Cat gave him the look and said, "Okay, now tell me who I should take today, Mr.

Handicapper? Hopefully, a horse faster than Stone Street."

After some consultation, it was decided to put Cat's $10 on the #4 entry, Awesome Gem that was 4 to 1 in the morning line.

I decided to go with an 8 to 1 long shot. An Irish import named Heatseeker, being ridden by Bijarano for a $20 to win. Heatseeker had been the subject of several write-ups on the Daily Racing Form web site.

With all our bets figured out, we headed for Canterbury Park for a day of horse racing.

When we got to the track, we lucked out with 2 pari-mutuel television screens open next to each other. Off Track betting facilities have small screens where you can pick up almost any track you want to bet on. They always have large screens on the wall showing the larger tracks and posting the live odds of the races being shown.

The first big race of the day's big four was the Golfstream Handicap. We watched a horse named Sir Whimsey win it paying $9.00. My bet, Fairbanks, came in second. Like they say, "Close, but no cigar."

The next big race was the 7th at Santa Anita, the Sham Stake. My trifecta box bet went into the toilet when Colonel John won, El Goto Molo placed, but Reflect the Times ran 4th, a $12 loss.

The next race was the Kilro Mile. My bet was $20 to win, $40 to place on Artiste Royal. Ever a Friend won it but my horse placed paying $7.00, giving me $140.00.

That put me well ahead going into the last race of the day, the Santa Anita Handicap. I had bet Cat's $10 on Awesome Gem and my $20 on Heetseeker. Stan had put his money on a horse named Go Between because his favorite jockey, Gomez, was in the saddle.

Heetseeker started his move at the top of the stretch and took the lead with one furlong to go. Stan's horse, Go Between, made a gallant effort in the last furlong, but my horse won it by nearly 2 lengths, paying $16.00. My $20 got me $160.00.

Cat's horse finished well back in the field, but, for us, it was a pretty good day.

We headed for the near-by Indian casino where I was happy to buy supper. While we ate, we flipped a coin to see who got the honor of telling Cat his 10 bucks was gone. Stan won the honor, most of the time a very unpleasant task.

The week passed and I didn't hear from Dawn. I decided to just wait and see what she decided to do about us. I sure did miss her companionship.

I still, periodically, went to visit my boy, Buddy's grave. Strange how I remembered so much about the little things he liked. He was like me and an avid reader.

I remember the night I took him to a book signing where he met John Sandford. That was a big night for him because he and I had both read all of Sandford's books.

It was early Tuesday morning when Stan called and asked if I would like to go to work with him. He was about to go looking for another warrant fugitive. I told him I sure would because boredom was setting in with Dawn gone and all.

Stan told me this guy was waiting for trial on 2 sexual assaults on a young girl in her teens. He didn't show for his trial and a warrant was issued. Our Bondsman was upset.

Stan had pretty good information from this guy's soon-to-be ex-wife as to where he could be located. His family had a cabin in northern Minnesota. It was on Big Round Lake, near the town of McGregor. This cabin was generally used only in the summer by this guy's elderly parents and had only a small wood stove for heat. She also told us he drove a red Saturn and loved to frequent local bars. As I've said, if you want information, talk to the local bartender.

We located the lake on the map. It was about 14 miles north and west of McGregor and about 5 miles from a little berg named Tamarack. About 2'ii hours later, we walked into a bar in McGregor. We asked the bartender if he knew the man we were looking for but he didn't. We asked if there was a bar in Tamarack, and he said there was.

He told us to talk to the owner of the bar and restaurant called the Village Pump.

His name was LaVerne Wilson. He said, "If anyone in Aitkin County can tell you the location of this dude you're looking for, it would be Wilson. Old Wilson is like the local legend up here."

So we headed east and about 15 minutes later, we spotted the Village Pump on the left. It was on the corner of the county road that would take us to Big Round Lake.

The bar was an old place but was clean and appeared well kept up. We asked the lady bartender for a beer and if LaVerne was around. He was and she went into the back to tell him we would like to see him.

LaVern, a short, slightly built man, came out and asked what it was we wanted.

We told him who we were looking for. He asked why we were looking for him. San told him we just had some business to take care of with him.

Then, to our surprise, a man who had been seated with his back to us at the bar turned around and said, "Must be some pretty serious business seeing as you're both carrying." He then reached into his pocket and showed us his ID and badge. He then asked us to show our permits to carry a concealed weapon. We showed him our permits and the papers on the man we were after. He checked them out and gave them back to us. He said to Vern, "They're alright, Vern." Then he got up and left.

"That is one customer I can't help but like," Vern said. "He has a place on Big Sandy Lake and stops in every once in a while."

"I believe it," I said, "That's a Federal badge he carries. Now can you help us out here, Vern?"

"Well, Vern said, "There is a guy that's been in quite a few times in the past couple of weeks who drives a red car. He said he was staying on the Big Round in a cabin his family owns. I don't know exactly where it is on Round." He added, "You might inquire at the Whispering Pines bar on Round. Just take county 6 out here for about 6 miles and it will come up on your left."

We thanked Vern and left. We did find Whispering Pines but didn't see a red Saturn. We didn't want to have him get a tip we were after him so decided to drive the roads around the lake and look for it.

We found it on the other side of the lake. As we pulled in behind it, someone was coming out of the cabin. When he saw us, he went back in and shut the door.

I told Stan I'd take the back. Drawing my gun, I proceeded around the cabin, staying well below the windows. I did notice the curtains moving and figured he now knew we were armed.

I just got settled behind a picnic table when I heard Stan yell, "You, in the cabin, come out with your hands up. We have a warrant for your arrest. Come out now with your hands in the air!"

Just a few seconds later, I heard a pistol shot and a shotgun blast go off almost together. I ran around the corner of the cabin and saw Stan on the ground, clutching his throat with a bloody hand.

The man from the cabin was on his knees trying to raise his shotgun toward Stan.

I shot him 3 times, knocking him over. He dropped the shotgun as he fell. I approached him and saw he was finished. The left side of his head was blown away.

I turned to Stan who was now on his knees and holding a bloody hand to his throat about where his neck and the bulletproof vest met. He tried to talk but couldn't.

I could see where the shotgun pellets had hit the tip of his vest. I laid him down and opened his shirt and vest. I could see where some of the pellets had missed the top of the vest and went into his throat about where his collar bone started. There were no exit wounds.

I called for an ambulance and told them our situation. I knew Stan's blood type and gave that to them also. I told Stan is wounds were not life threatening. It was lucky for him no major throat artery appeared severed.

Then I called the county Sheriff s office and was told to stay put and they would be at the scene in 10 minutes. As always, we had called them before we started after our man. They had checked us out and given us the go-ahead.

Two county squads arrived within minutes. They collected all firearms. One pair tried to help Stan and the other pair put me in the squad car.

About then, the medics arrived and quickly loaded Stan up and started to work on him. I was taken to the Aitkin County Sheriff's office and gave them a statement. I was put in a holding cell but was allowed to use the phone and made some calls.

The first call was to the hospital to check on Stan. He was doing well and was being operated on to remove small pellets. Lucky for Stan the guy didn't have buckshot in that gun because he would be gone.

The next call was to my lawyer. Earl said he would be up in the morning and assured me he would have me out in a few hours.

Before lockdown I again called Stan and, to my surprise, got hold of him in his room. He said he would be released in the morning and would come to the jail.

Things went about as Earl said they would, and I was released about 10:00. Stan got there about then and we headed back to the Cities after calling the bondsman and filling him in.

I went back to work at the gunsmith shop. I figured Stan and I wouldn't have any bail jumpers to run down for a while and Stan needed some time to heal.

One afternoon, a .45 auto was brought in to be fixed, an old Colt M-1911. It was just like my old favorite that Stan had thrown into the river. I sure missed that gun. I installed the needed part and called to tell the owner the gun was done and I wanted him to ask for me when he picked it up. He came in the next day and asked for me. I told him what I did to fix his gun and asked if he would sell it.

At first he said, "No, I've had it for years and like it." Then I said, "I'll give you $300.00 for it." He thought about it for a minute, then handed it to me butt first. "Sold," he said. Apparently he needed money more than the gun.

When I had to turn in my old .45 I had kept the silencer. I got to work making a new barrel threaded to hold the silencer. It took a while to make the new barrel, adjust the sight and set the trigger pull to my liking. It was great having my old .45 back.

Saturday morning rolled around. I picked up the Daily Racing Form and headed for the Lounge to meet up with Stan. My old spot at the end of the bar was open and Cat had my beer there when I sat down. I had noticed a horse racing fact in one of the racing papers and, knowing how Cat loved to hear off-the-wall horse racing facts, I laid one on him.

"Cat," I said, "Do you know the name of the first all-white horse to be registered as a thoroughbred?"

"Here we go, lay it on me," Cat replied.

"She was a filly named White Beauty that was foaled in 1963." Cat responded by walking away muttering something about useless information.

Stan happened to be coming down the bar about that time and overheard Cat's muttering. He asked me, "What the hell was that all about?" I told him and we both had a good laugh.

We opened up the racing form and got down to work. Two big races were being run today. The Tampa Bay Derby had a heavy favorite at 1 to 9 in the morning line. His name was War Pass and had never been beat with an impressive string of 5 victories.

However, he was going against tougher horses than he had ever run against in the past. I liked the horse named Big Trunk and decided I would put $20 on him to win. Cat and Stan decided to take a horse named Atoned, also a good bet.

The second big race was at Santa Anita. I picked Bob Black Jack in the San Filipi and Stan went with Georgie Boy.

Well, they were off. In the Tampa Bay race, the favorite did not go off at 1 to 9.

Guess who finished dead last but the favorite War Pass. I guess his time had passed. My pick won the race. Big Truck won it and Stan and Cat's horse, Atoned, finished a neck behind him. Big Truck paid a whopping $16.40, so I picked up a nice $164.00 at the window.

At Santa Anita my pick, Bob Black Jack, lost to Stan's pick, Georgie Boy which was no surprise because they were the 2 favorites in the race.

I was at the window making some bets when I noticed Dawn a couple of windows down. She was with a tall man who was being very attentive. They were going over some racing sheets while they waited in line. It looked to me like she had found someone to share her new interest in handicapping horses. I went back to my seat and watched the last 2 races with kind of a lack of interest.

As we were leaving, Dawn came up behind me and said, "Elroy, meet my brother, Dick." Turning to Dick she said, "Dick, this is the mystery man you've been wanting to meet." Shaking his hand I said, "Nice to meet you. I didn't know Dawn had a brother."

Dawn said, "Well I do and you and him have a lot in common. He is a retired policeman, too, from Chicago. He is looking to move back here where we grew up."

"Well, Dick, I hope you find what you're looking for here. You have a wonderful sister."

"Yes, I know I do," he replied, "Which is partly why I'm glad we ran into you.

Dawn and I are very close and when one of us has a problem, we don't hesitate to ask for help. Now how about we go some place and have a drink and talk over her problem?"

"Where would you like to go?" I asked. "Let's meet at Katie's," Dawn suggested.

"That's fine with me," I replied. "I'll see you there."

On the way I thought about what was going to happen. I was sure her cop brother would want to know all about what I had been accused of. He would for sure ask why I can't tell the whole story to Dawn.

About all I could tell him is what I already told Dawn about never revealing the other people involved.

They got to Katie's in Arden Hills before me and were seated in a rear booth. I joined them and ordered drinks. Dick asked me how I had done at the track, and I told him not too well.

We continued to make small talk mostly about our police careers. Finally I started it off by saying, "Well, Dick, as I told Dawn, I can't tell you anything about the charges I was found not guilty of. There are other people involved who could be hurt if the whole story becomes public. It's all in the past now and must, I repeat, must stay in the past."

"Well," Dick said, "My sister thinks the world of you. But she feels you were some way involved in some killings. If you were, she needs to know. So if you were but refuse to tell her the whole story, I believe it should end here for you two. A lasting relationship is built on trust and can't survive without it. So tell us and Dawn will make her decision about the future of you two or get up and walk away."

I got up, took out my wallet and put $20.00 on the table, more than enough to cover the drinks. I said, "I am truly sorry," as I walked away. I drove home and picked up a box of ammo for my new .45 and drove to an indoor gun range. Shooting always took my mind off things. I shot up the box continuing to get the feel of the gun. I ended it with a nice tight pattern.

I stopped and had a couple of beers, then headed home in time to catch the news.

There was a story about a court case against a man who had shot another man over a supposed drug deal that had gone bad. The reason for releasing the charged man was the 2 eye witnesses the state was going to use to convict the man, had disappeared. I thought to myself, they were either dead or were running after receiving death threats against them or their families.

They showed a photo of the accused man and it got my attention. It was the bodyguard of the man I had shot near the White Castle on University and Snelling Avenues. I recalled how he had left his boss on the ground while he drove away munching on his boss's hamburgers. Apparently he was now in charge of the boss's gang.

I wished now I had taken him out when I got his boss. I probably would have saved the lives of 2 people, the 2 people who had failed to show in court.

His name was Tyrone Willis. Using my old police connections, I found out he was the new gang leader. Also the gang had grown since he had taken over. They were quickly gaining a bad reputation for numerous assaults and shootings in the old St. Paul midway area. Yes, the midway area, my old hunting grounds. All this brought back thoughts of my boy. God how I missed my Buddy! Scum like this gang went on destroying lives while my Buddy was lying in his grave.

During that long and sleepless night, I came to a decision. I just couldn't let people like Tyrone Willis continue to defy the law. Swine like him killed my boy.

Somehow, some way, I would set him up and be prosecuted and put away. Set him up so there would be no way he could beat the rap. This way, I would keep my word to Stan that there would be no more killings. In fact, I would ask Stan to help me.

CHAPTER 16

I called Stan the next morning and told him what I was going to do. He thought it was a great idea.

I got started by getting Tyrone's address from the police gang unit. He lived on Randolph Street in St. Paul's midway area. I still had Buddy's car so I could switch between his and mine, making it harder to spot me while I was parked near Tyrone's house and made my plans.

The first few nights I noted the same 2 vehicles were parked in his driveway overnight, a black Lincoln and a black Lexus SUV. Two men always left together early in the evening in the Lexus and returned about 2:00 a.m.

They carried a small canvas bag with them. I assumed it contained drugs and cash to resupply their street people. It had to have been packaged somewhere after being broken down. I planned to find out where.

Tyrone never left the house during the first 4 nights. When he left during the day, it was always with this big dude. The big guy always drove and opened the doors for Tyrone. I noticed the big guy always wore a jacket or long sleeve shirts, even on warm nights, and never tucked his shirt in. I figured he was carrying and, more than likely, so was Tyrone.

Then Friday night came and everything changed. The Lexus left but about an hour later it returned and Tyrone and his bodyguard got in the back seat. When they left, I followed at a safe distance. They made about 20 stops in all, about half of them along University Avenue. The rest were at various corners in downtown St. Paul.

Saturday night was about the same as Friday night—the same stops and the exchanges of small bags that contained drugs or cash.

Sunday came and they went back to the weeknight routine. Tyrone and the bodyguard stayed in but did have an occasional visit from females.

I got together with Stan to see if he agreed with what I had seen going down could be a perfect set-up or not. He agreed but said we had to make finding the location where they were getting their drug supply from, our top priority. The next night he joined me. We talked it over and agreed that late on Saturday night would be the best time to hit Tyrone's house, right after both cars had returned for the night. Surely there would be enough drugs and money to jail the whole organization.

The only way to find where their drug supply was coming from was to follow them. We decided to follow them Monday night and, using 2 cars, we would keep switching, making it hard to spot us. Stan had a good pair of walkie-talkies with a range of several miles so we could communicate as we followed them.

Monday night we were ready. The Lexus left at their normal time, and I was about 2 blocks behind them. They headed downtown and when they got there, Stan and I switched cars.

They pulled into a parking ramp on Kellogg Blvd. Stan called me and told me they had parked on the lower level. I found them and parked where I could watch them without them seeing me.

Twice a Ford pickup dove by them slowly, checking the cars in the area to see if any were occupied. The 3rd time, the pickup stopped and the passenger got out with a small canvas bag in his hand. He gave the bag to the passenger in the Lexus who gave him something that I couldn't see.

I called Stan and he got their license number as they left the parking ramp. We then decided to call it a night and met at the Savoy, a bar on 7th Street for a drink and to talk it over. We decided to take everything we had to the Drug Enforcement division the next morning.

We met with them and gave them all our information. They were very impressed! They agreed that a Saturday morning might be the best time to hit Tyrone's operation.

They were very interested in that pickup truck that was apparently the supplier.

Looking back now, I wish we had followed it. We might have found their drug lab.

As we expected, we were told to stay out of it from this point on. We knew they would run that truck plate and get an address. But we were out of it so we left it in their hands, although it was hard to do.

CHAPTER 17

The following Saturday morning found us in our usual place in the Lounge.

When Cat brought us our drinks, Stan loudly said, "Cat, did you know a guy named James Rowe has registered 10 Belmont wins, 8 as a trainer and 2 as a jockey in 1872 and 1873?"

Cat looked at us and said, "You two should find a quiz show with horse racing as the question subject and get rich. However, in the meantime pick me a winner." He then put $10 on the bar to cover his bet for the day.

On the way to the track, our plans changed when we got a call from the Bail Bondsman. He wanted us to go after a man who had jumped bail and missed a court appearance to answer a charge of theft from the state office where he worked. He was accused of stealing over ten grand.

He lived in an apartment in North St. Paul, a community just to the northeast of St. Paul. His landlord told us he hadn't seen Dickie since the first day he went to court.

We next checked the office where he worked or used to work. We were told he was a real loner. He was divorced and never had any children. His EX had left the area some time ago.

It was beginning to appear this was not going to be an easy man to locate when we got lucky with one individual who told us our man was a huge hockey fan and had season tickets for the Minnesota Wild. The Wild had a home game scheduled for the coming Wednesday night. We got our guy's seat number and bought ourselves tickets to the game. I was always a big hockey fan myself and was looking forward to Wednesday night.

We got to the game and informed security. They showed us where his seat was and we found a good spot to watch it and not be noticed. About 10 minutes before game time, our man showed. Stan went in one end of his seat row and I stood at the other end. Just before Stan reached him, he figured something was up and started toward me.

Just before he got to me, I opened my coat and showed him my .45. He stopped and raised his hands. I motioned him forward and when he reached the aisle, I turned him and cuffed him. Stan joined us and we left to turn him in at the city jail.

We called the bondsman and told him his man was in jail. Then we headed out to have a few drinks to celebrate our collar. Turns out the Wild hockey game was on the bar's television, so we got to watch most of the 3rd period before calling it a night.

To our surprise, the morning paper had a big story about a big shootout during a major drug bust. Sure enough, it was our boy, Tyrone. The police had raided his home and 3 of his boys had been shot. Tyrone had somehow either escaped or was not there when the police hit. Either way, he was now on the run with a federal reward for his capture or information about his location. Stan called me after he had seen the paper and told me it was the federal drug force that had handled the raid on Tyrone's house. They were now in charge because our information on the pickup truck that was the supplier's had led them to uncover a national drug operation.

Then Stan said, "Elroy, I think we are back on the case." I asked, "What do you mean?"

"Well, Buddy, it seems the feds posted a $20,000 reward for information leading to Tyrone's arrest."

"Well, well, here we go again," I replied. "This could be a wild one. Where do you want to start, Stan?"

"I think we start this afternoon. We'll run down some of our old informants. We just might get lucky and pick up a tip or two. It will cost us a few bucks, but twenty grand is twenty grand."

That evening I picked up Stan and we headed for the usual low life hangouts. We talked to maybe a dozen different guys and they were very reluctant to discuss Tyrone or any of his people. Several of those we talked to said we were dead wrong if we thought Tyrone was out of business.

Other than just letting a bunch of them enjoy a few free drinks at our expense, we learned very little about Tyrone's location. We could tell they still had a lot of respect or maybe it was fear of what Tyrone would do to anyone giving out any information about him.

We called it a night after checking about 10 bars and numerous hangouts to no avail. About 11:00 that night, the phone rang as I was about to hit the shower. A man asked, "You the guy trying to find Tyrone?"

I said, "Yes, I am. What about it?"

The man told me to bring $100 the next night to the parking lot off Kellogg under the end of the Lafayette Bridge. He added, "And bring along that buddy of yours."

I told him we would be there. My first thought was Tyrone had gotten the word we were trying to locate him. This was a set-up.

I called Stan and told him about the call. When I finished, he said, "A set-up if ever I heard one."

I told him I agreed and we had better come up with a plan of our own to use their plan to our advantage.

Stan asked if I still had my service vest. I told him, "Hell yes and 3 extra clips for my .45!"

"Then it's a go," Stan replied. "We will get there real early in separate cars with our hand-held radios and watch them set up their ambush. With any luck, maybe Tyrone will be there. If so, we can finish this thing."

After Stan hung up, I cleaned the old .45 and dug out my old bullet-proof vest. I started to think about my boy, Buddy. I said aloud, "Well, Buddy, if we get this guy, a lot of drugs will be off the street—at least for a while."

CHAPTER 18

The Lafayette Bridge crosses the Mississippi River to the east of downtown and lands in an area called West St. Paul. Under the bridge on the St. Paul side where the meet was to be, there is a large parking area.

Stan and I arrived well before dark in separate cars. Stan went in first and drove around the lot. He called me and said he hadn't seen anyone and had found a place to park where he could observe the area.

I entered the lot and Stan, on the two-way radio, guided me to about 50 yards from him.

We waited.

About when we thought they were no-shows, a black van arrived and parked just inside the entrance. One man got out and walked toward me, but between car rows, hunched down trying not to be seen. He stopped about 10 cars from me. On the trunk of the car he was behind, he laid down what looked like an M-16.

I quietly called Stan on the two-way and told him where he was and what I was going to do. I slipped out of my car and, staying low, crept to within 3 cars of him. I stood up racking my .45 and said, "Touch that gun and you're dead!"

He turned toward me and saw the .45 pointed at him. He slowly stepped back and raised his hands without being told. I knew we were far enough away from his black van so we couldn't be seen by his buddies, if we stayed low getting back to my car. I checked him and found a small hand gun tucked in his belt. I cuffed him and told him to stay quiet and low and started him back to my car. I put him in the trunk, closed it, and called Stan again and told him I had one in my trunk. I told him I was going to check the van and see how many more there are and click my radio button to give the count.

Stan said, "Okay but be damned careful." It turned out I didn't have to be that careful. They must have thought we weren't coming because there were 3 of them and they had the radio on pretty loud.

I got back a ways and called Stan. We agreed to take them and quickly made a plan. Stan started his car and pulled up to the front of the black van, skidding to a stop.

All 3 of them got out of the van. The one from the passenger side had a large handgun he was holding by the back of his leg.

Stan said, "You guys looking for us?"

The van driver said, "Ya, where is your buddy?"

"Right here, drop that gun or I drop you," I shouted as I stood up pointing my .45 across the hood of the car next to them, startling the hell out of them. The one with the gun dropped it and they both raised their hands.

Stan got out of his car and searched the 2 of them. He found a small handgun on the driver. He hit him across the face with it, dropping him to the ground.

Stan shouted, "Now where the hell is Tyrone?" One of the men replied, "Go to hell." Stan kicked him hard and again asked, "Where's Tyrone?"

I picked up the other man and kneed him. He went back down yelling in pain. The other one said, "Tyrone will kill the both of you."

"Well," Stan said, "At least now we know Tyrone sent you."

We got them both on their feet and I put my .45 into the ear of one and said, "Stan, I'm going to shoot this clown. Then maybe his buddy will see we mean business and tell us where their boss is."

"Okay," the one I had my gun on said. "I'll tell you where Tyrone is. Just don't shoot me"

"Shut up!" his buddy ordered.

But he told us and we called in the police. We told them the whole story and they picked up Tyrone.

We met at the Lounge to celebrate the night we got the money. It was Friday and we were loaded and ready to hit the track the next day. It was going to be a big day for racing!

Eight big money races in what was called The Sunshine Millions. It consisted of 4 big races at Golfstream for a purse total of $2,000,000 dollars. There were also 4 races at Santa Anita for another $1,550,000 dollars.

We hit the track in time for the 1st Golfstream race with a purse of $250,000.

The 11th entry, You Lucky Mann was the favorite at 5 to 2. We decided to put Cat's $5 on him.

I decided to trifecta box that horse with Backbackbackgone, the number 2 horse and the number 1 horse, Southern Exchange.

The 2nd race was a filly and mare turf going 1 1/8th for $500,000 dollars. In this one we just put Cat's $5 on the morning favorite, Wild Promises. Stan and I both put that horse with Zee Zee and Bel Air Sizzle.

The 3rd race was filly and mare sprint. Cat's bet went on the favorite, Dearest Trickski. I boxed an Exacta with Mystical Plan and Lovely Isle.

The 4th race was the big Classic, one and one eighth miles on the dirt for $1,000,000. What I did not like about this race was the big field of 14 entries, 6 of them going off at 20 to 1. Big fields could mean a good horse could get trapped and lose the race. We put Cat's $5 on Delightful Kiss at 3 to 1. I also took him with Dry Martini and It's A Bird for a trifecta box.

We then switched to Santa Anita. The first of the 4 big races was the 8th, a turf race for 4 year olds and up for $500,000.00. Again, the dreaded crowded field of 14 entries, 6 of them at 20 or 30 to 1.

Cat's bet went on the favorite, Soldiers Dancer. I put a $20 to win bet and $40 to place on Icy Atlantic who was 9 to 2 in the morning line.

The 2nd big race was the Santa Anita Oaks, a 6 furlong filly race for $250,000.00 with 9 entries. Cat's bet went on the favorite, Emmy Darling at 3 to 1. I bet the same horse to win for $20.00.

The 3rd big race was the sprint, 6 furlongs for 4 year olds and up for $300,000.00. Again, Cat's bet went on the favorite, Georgie Boy. I put $20 on the same horse to win.

The 4th and last big money race was the Distaff, fillies and mares running for $500,000.00. Cat's bet went on the favorite again, a horse named Leah's Secret. In this one I took a long shot, Bai Bai for $20 to win and $40 to place.

Stan and I settled back to watch the Sunshine Millions on the screens at Canterbury Park with betting tickets in hand and high hopes.

A few hours later, when all was said and done, Cat had won the 8th at Golfstream, the 6th, the 8th, and the 9th at Santa Anita. Because of making all short odds bets, he won only $49.00.

I hit my trifecta at Golfstream winning $183.00 and the 8th for another $66.00.

Stan sad he had a fair day with about $46.00 ahead. We headed for the Lounge and a few victory cocktails.

CHAPTER 19

It sure was nice having that extra cash from that reward check. Ten grand is a lot of dough for an old retired cop. I got the car tuned up and some new tires. I paid some bills and relaxed with no money worries for a change.

I couldn't help but think about Dawn from time to time. I couldn't help but think about what might have been.

The following Friday, Stan really surprised me. He told me he had taken a job in Chicago. He was going to work for a private investigator he had known for years. He said he was bored and needed to have some action.

We went out to dinner as kind of a farewell. After we ate, we were on the way to our cars when Stan stopped me. He took my hand and said, "Elroy, we have been friends for a hell of a long time. We have saved each other's ass more than once. I want you to forget that promise you made me about your pursuit of drug peddlers. We probably won't see each other again so have at it, if that's what you want. I know how much the loss of your son haunts you so do what you must. You're one of the smartest guys I know, so be careful and stay safe."

I looked at Stan's departing car and realized my best friend was leaving. I went home and went over the memories of the times Stan and I had spent together both at work and socially. I remember what his friendship meant to me when my Buddy was killed.

When Stan released me from my promise to stop taking revenge on dope dealers, I knew I would begin again, and I was back cruising the streets at night. The 3rd night I found what I was looking for.

I watched him work his corner until midnight. I came back the next few nights and saw his repeat business was pretty good. Two cars and a pickup truck stopped and did a transaction several times each night. I believe they were reselling his product.

This guy was pretty careful. He had lookouts 1 block to the north and 1 block to the south near the college campus along Snelling Avenue. They talked by walkie talkie and about mid-night he would call them and pick them up closing down business for the night.

This was a fairly busy traffic area so it was going to be a problem taking him out without being seen. If I just drove up and shot him through the car window someone might see him fall.

I decided the way to do it was to park on a side street and walk up to him then shooting him between some parked cars so no one would see him fall.

I was dressed in my old timers outfit with an old jacked with big deep pockets. One of which held my silenced .45.

When I got close to him I held out my left hand with some bills in it.

He looked at me and said, "What you want old man?"

"Some of that good tobacco I know you are selling, "I replied.

He reached into his jacket pocket for what I thought would be some drugs but when his hand started to come out I saw the handle of a handgun. I leveled my .45 at him and told him to drop the gun.

He said, "I figured drugs weren't all you were after."

I said, "Wrong again and shot him twice in the chest. On his way down he said, "Fooled by an old—"

I checked the lookouts and they were both doing business . . .

I went through his pockets and got his large bankroll. Then I rolled him under a parked car.

I got to my car and drove by the scene. Two cars were stopped and people were looking at the body.

The two body guards were running toward the scene.

I headed for home thinking of the things I had better do if the police showed up at my house when they found the dead dope seller shot with a .45. First I had to wash my clothes and take a shower to get all gun residue off me and hide the .45 until I could change barrels again.

On the way home, as always after a shooting, my thoughts turned to my Buddy. I guess, in some strange way, my shooting these punks seemed justified—righteous kills. The world of good people didn't need them or their dope ruining young people's lives.

The shooting happened too late to make the morning papers. The next day the paper had only a short article on it. They got it right because they reported it as a drug related shooting. To my relief and surprise, I didn't hear anything from the police that day.

I figured they hadn't processed the slugs yet or didn't suspect me. This I found hard to believe after all I had been through.

It was Saturday morning so I picked up the Daily Racing Form and headed for the Lounge. I just couldn't let go of Stan's ritual of laying a horse racing fact on Cat every Saturday. It was up to me to carry on the tradition.

I settled in at my usual spot at the end of the bar and loudly called out to Cat to bring me a beer. The usual Saturday morning crowd was there and they turned toward me, knowing what was coming.

When Cat got to me, I loudly asked, "Cat, what horse paid the lowest odds ever after winning the Preakness?"

Cat said, "How the hell would I know, Elroy?"

I said, "Citation. He paid only $11 for a $10 bet." My answer received the usual smattering of applause.

"Fine," Cat said, "Now pick me a winner in the big race today," and put $10 on the bar.

I told him his bet was going on West Side Bernie, the morning line odds second pick . . .

Well, it ended up long-shot day at Turfway Park for the Lane's End. Hold Me Back won it paying $22.20.

Flying Private ran second paying $22.60.

Proceed Bee showed paying $9.60.

As handicappers say, "That's horse racing." I knew Cat had watched the race on ESPN so I figured I didn't have to stop and tell him his money was gone.

I figured it would be no big surprise to see a squad car in my driveway when I got home. I did get a surprise when I got there. Dawn was just pulling away. I honked my horn and she stopped and got out. I invited her in and she accepted.

She asked if I had just come from the track, and I told her all about my bad day at the track.

She gave me a kiss on the cheek and said, "You can't always come home a winner. How about we go out for dinner?"

We dined at Povlitski's in nearby Spring Lake Park. Over dinner we made small talk about horse handicapping. When we finished, she asked if we could go back to my place and talk. I said sure and one the way, I realized how happy I was to be spending time with her again. She had my heart in her hands.

We talked for hours. In the end we both admitted we had the same feelings for one another. We came to an agreement to forget the past and start fresh.

I wanted her to spend the night, but she said, "You can count on it next time."

After she left, I thought about her and if Buddy would have liked her. I somehow knew he would have.

I made my final decision about this revenge thing. It was finished. It was over. Time for a new life. Time to begin again and by God, I would make it work!